A YEAR OF SHORT FICTION

2025 STONE'S THROW

FROM ROCK AND A HARD PLACE

STONE'S THROW EDITOR: Morgan Sullivan
STONE'S THROW ANNUAL EDITOR: Jay Butkowski
RHP EDITOR-IN-CHIEF: Roger Nokes
CONTRIBUTING EDITOR: Albert Tucher
EDITOR: Paul J. Garth
EDITOR: Rob D. Smith
ACQUISITION EDITOR: Ashley-Ruth M. Bernier
ACQUISITION EDITOR: Victor De Anda
ACQUISITION EDITOR: Susan Jessen
GUARDIAN ANGEL: Jonathan Elliott
COVER DESIGNER: Heather Garth

ON THE WEB: **www.rockandahardplacemag.com**
BY EMAIL: **editors@rockandahardplacemag.com**

Rock and a Hard Place Magazine is a labor of love, produced by a team of volunteer editors to showcase the best in dark fiction, crime, dystopian fiction, and noir. To learn how you can support the mission of **Rock and a Hard Place Press** through tax-deductible donations, or by subscribing to the RHP Patreon, please visit the website, and click "**Support RHP**" through the main menu.

Print ISBN: 979-8-9938836-1-8

eBook ISBN: 979-8-9938836-2-5

Published by Rock and a Hard Place Press, an imprint of Rock and a Hard Place Press, LLC, Woodbridge, NJ.
rockandahardplacemag.com
amazon.com/Rock-and-a-Hard-Place-Press

Follow us on Social Media:
https://www.facebook.com/RHP.books/
https://www.instagram.com/rhp.press/
https://www.threads.net/@rhp.press
https://bsky.app/profile/rhppress.bsky.social
https://x.com/RHP_Press

Contents

Foreword: Prompting Excellence

Jay Butkowski

The best laid plans of mice and men . . .

So, we'll start with a peak behind the curtain: **Rock and a Hard Place Press** is what one of our editors lovingly calls a "punk rock collective," which means that we're guided by DIY values, and any one of us can pick up and do a thing when something needs to get done. It means we all get to take part in shaping this publishing venture with our own creative lens, our own inspirations, and our own aesthetic, melding it and merging it with the ideas and vision and creativity of the other members on our editorial board.

The rotating duties of prompt-giver for *Stone's Throw* are a perfect example of this collective approach in action. Each year, we try to assign someone to take the lead on the coming year's *Stone's Throw* prompts, with input and feedback given by the rest of the editorial panel.

And 2025 was my turn in the barrel.

At the end of last year, I was looking at a blank page (and as I write this foreword, I'll note its similarity to the one staring at—and mocking—me now), with the intention to fill it with prompts that would elicit **Stone's Throw** literary genius for the coming year. I infused the prompts with topical references, inside jokes, and my own brand of irreverence and sarcasm. And the other editors let me run with it.

Heading into the new year, I knew the types of stories I wanted to get, based on the types of stories *I* would write given the same prompt. It felt good (and a little indulgent) to get my thumbprints all up on a year's worth of short crime fiction and noir, even if I didn't get the byline.

The writers who showed up surprised the hell out of me.

That's not to say that each story didn't relate back to the prompt. They all did, just not in the way *I* would have written it. And in several cases, I stood back, scratched my head, and said, "Oh, shit . . . I didn't think about it *that* way." Each writer took the prompt I handed down, and knocked it out of the park, even if it wasn't what I originally had in mind.

And as a result, you've got stories about a stripper-turned fight pro-moter and man-children fighting moose. Of pyramid-scheme come-uppance and a badass Queer protagonist turning the tables on her abusers. Of avenging moms and a mother who teaches her daughter the value in standing up for herself. Of an aging pop-punk caught in a fame spiral, and a domestic violence survivor who finds freedom amidst the flames. Of heartbreaking coming of age, and grief that endures, and unending faith in a war zone.

And "Santa Daddy," a story so horny that I hope my mother doesn't read it (though I personally loved it!).

It's humbling to see how the prompts that came out of my brain turned into the stories that came out of theirs. It reminds me of the philosophy underpinning **Rock and a Hard Place**, that the sum of the creative whole is greater than the value of each of its component parts.

It also feels a little like my experiences being a dad—you teach them, and guide them, and point them in a direction, but ultimately, the kids are going to find their own way. And that's what's supposed to happen. And even though it might not be the way you would have chosen, you're still proud as hell that they found something that is true and authentic to themselves.

I'm proud of this annual issue of ***Stone's Throw***, and grateful to each of the writers who elevated my prompts into memorable slices of noir and crime fiction.

It's not how I would have written it. It's better. And that's the whole point.

-Jay Butkowski
Managing Editor
December 2025

For the **RHP** board: Roger, Morgan, Al, Paul, Rob, Victor, Ashley, Susan, and Jonathan

JANUARY 2025 PROMPT – The holidays are over, and it's time to get back on the straight and narrow. Easier said than done, though. This month, we want stories about overindulgence. Opulence. Living beyond your means. Whether that's money, drugs, generosity, or viciousness, we want stories about people who overdo it, and what happens when they realize they're in a hole they can't hope to fill.

Tempting Destiny

Lisa Robertson

When I got on the Greyhound to Las Vegas, my grandpa sent me off with $825 and three unbreakable rules:

1. Make your own destiny.

2. Pay for everything in cash.

3. Never trust a southpaw.

The money didn't last long, but the advice stuck with me, and—for the most part—it's served me well. That doesn't mean I don't slip up sometimes. I've learned that when you break one or even two of Grandpa's rules, it's not a big deal. But when you manage to complete the trifecta, you might find yourself in one jackpot of a crisis.

Grandpa didn't need to tell me to make my own destiny—that's something I've done naturally all my life. It's right there in my name. You have to be a self-starter with a name like Destineé.

I always thought my destiny was to be a showgirl at one of the big casinos—the classy kind with feathered headdresses and sequined pasties. I've been working towards this dream my whole life. I started taking classes at Miss Althea's School of Dance at two. I was captain of the varsity kick line all four years of high school. That's unprecedented.

But in Vegas it doesn't matter how fast you pick up choreography or how flexible you are. To be in a fancy show, you gotta be at least a hundred feet tall, have huge tits and an ass you can bounce a quarter off of.

Fail. Fail. And fail.

At my sixth audition, a choreographer told me the only way I would ever dance on the Strip was if I was spinning around a pole.

I didn't leave Oklahoma to become a stripper. I could've done that back in Tahlequah. But if you want to control your own destiny, you don't tuck your tail beneath what that choreographer called "a truly colossal ass" and get on a bus headed home. No, you suck up your pride, get hired on the day shift at Boobapalooza and start saving all those rolled up twenties.

Boobapalooza is like the Denny's of titty bars: super-focused on volume, less concerned with quality. We've got a $7.77 surf-and-turf lunch special and $20 lap dances from 2-4. Customers won't needle you too much if they're getting a ribeye and lobster tail for under ten bucks and the opportunity to motorboat a stripper for twenty. We are straight-up packed around the clock.

Of course, to make real money on the day shift, you gotta hustle. Smile a lot. Throw your hair around. Act halfway in love with every guy that even thinks about looking your way.

The best part is that the fruit of all that labor gets delivered in cash—that's a bonus when it comes to rule number two. I paid for my boob job in cash. These full Cs got me promptly promoted to the twilight shift where the real magic happens.

In most titty bars, the best strategy is having regulars. But in Vegas, it's mostly tourists. Finding a regular here is like finding a unicorn. And when you do find one, you better lock that horn down.

My unicorn's name? Mr. Louie.

Every girl in Vegas—stripper or not—knows some version of Mr. Louie. An older guy with a shiny suit, gold nugget jewelry and a very sketchy employment history. They tend to brand themselves as entrepreneurs. It's no coincidence that entrepreneur rhymes with manure—these guys are mostly full of shit.

What makes Mr. Louie different is that even though he looks and acts like a million other Guy Fieri wannabes, he has the cash to back up his play. Plus, he's got a fully exploitable soft spot for ambitious girls from Oklahoma.

Mr. Louie hands out hundreds the way you would give a puppy a treat when it finally pees outside. He's had three heart attacks, so he avoids lap dances like the plague. Mostly he just likes to talk: about the people he knows and the stuff he owns. I spend a lot of time listening, asking questions, and looking fascinated.

To be honest, Mr. Louie is kind of fascinating. Because for someone without a job, he has a lot of cash. When I first met him, he claimed to be a boxing coach, but I knew that was a lie. After a couple of months, Mr. Louie asked me if I wanted to know how he really made his money.

Yes. Yes, I did.

Turns out, he was involved in boxing, but not as a coach. He fixed fights. And he started telling me which ones to bet on. Betting on a fight—even a fixed one—is not for the faint of heart. Sometimes boxers get squirrely. Or word gets out, too much money gets bet and the whole thing gets called off. According to Mr. Louie, the trick is to not bet more than you can afford to lose. Start small. Build a bankroll. Keep it to yourself. Always play the long game.

It's good advice, but it sure is hard to follow. There's a lot of temptation in this town. I'm not stupid. I know stripping is not a job I can retire from—there's no 401(k). So, it's been a relief to find a side hustle that doesn't involve gyrating in a thong. I've been looking for the right fight with the right odds for a long time. When I finally found it, I decided to go all in.

***

Mr. Louie liked to bring the guys he worked with into the club. He was always introducing me to some promoter or manager or fighter, asking me to show them a good time. To me, they were just guys to grind on. I didn't think too much about them until heavyweight contender and all-around hottie Benji "Get Some Action" Jackson sauntered into Boobapalooza.

Boxers are not attractive dudes. They've got those awful cauliflower ears, and getting punched in the head all the time doesn't do a whole lot for their intellect either. But Benji? 205 pounds of solid muscle with high cheekbones and skin the color of coffee with just one splash of cream. Nevada doesn't get a whole lot of earthquakes, but the ground surely moved when that man walked into my life.

When Mr. Louie introduced us, Benji took my hand and said, "Destineé? With a name like that, I should make you part of mine." Guys say stupid shit like that to me all the time. But when Benji said it with his slow Georgia drawl, I was done. I didn't even care that it was his left hand that he extended.

Benji and I didn't slow roll it, and we didn't try to hide it either. If it bothered Mr. Louie, he didn't say anything. He had a lot invested in Benji, and he said it was in both our best interests to keep Benji happy. So, I did.

Being left-handed is a big advantage for boxers. Benji was legit—ranked eighth in the world and due for a title fight. But last week, Mr. Louie told Benji he had to throw his next fight.

The fight in question . . . not a good one to lose. It was against a straight-up chump from an Eastern European country with hardly any vowels. He's fat. He's slow. His training regimen consists of vodka and Eurotrash hookers named Katarzyna. The guy hasn't won a fight in two years. If Benji lost to him, he'd lose his shot at the belt, too.

And while this was bad news for Benji, it was great news for me. I didn't want to piss Benji off by betting against him, but I figured a $300K payday to take a dive in the fifth ought to be enough to soften any blow to his pride.

When Mr. Louie tells you to lose, you lose, and since Benji couldn't say no, I saw no reason not to say yes.

The only problem was with my bankroll. Or lack thereof. I had recently "invested" in some pretty dumb shit. Mostly designer handbags, bottle service and a quarter partnership in a hydroponic marijuana grow house on the north side. The good news was I paid cash for everything. The bad news? I didn't have any cash left—just some weak weed and a couple cute purses.

This fight was a once-in-a-lifetime thing. Usually, the odds are like three to two, maybe five to one if you're lucky. Benji was favored 40 to 1. Forty to one—that's Tyson-Douglas odds.

When opportunity knocks, smart girls answer the door.

I went all in. Maxed out every credit card I had with the biggest cash advances I could get. And I put every cent of it on the chump. Benji said he understood. Between what he'd make from throwing the fight and how much I stood to win from betting on it, we'd be set.

Mr. Louie and I sat right down front on fight night as Benji's special guests. When Benji came to the ring in his gold lamé robe with black leather trim and "Get Some Action" embroidered on the back, he looked like a biracial Elvis.

His opponent looked like a beachball with legs. Benji was supposed to dance around the guy until the fifth, let him get in one good punch then take a dive.

This should have been the big score we'd been waiting for, but destiny had a mind of its own that night. I guess, technically, it was Benji with the mind of his own. Because right at the opening bell, the love of my life jogged right over to the chump, yelled "always bet on black" and clocked the guy with an uppercut from that big old left hand of his.

Talk about a sucker punch.

Fifty thousand dollars in 15 seconds. That's what I lost. I can't imagine what Benji was thinking. And it's not like I can ask him, cause in all the commotion, he hightailed it back to the dressing room and right out the backdoor. Rumor has it he's waiting for things to blow over in Mexico. I sure hope Montezuma's isn't the only revenge he's getting served down there.

I still got off a lot easier than poor Mr. Louie. He tried to rush the ring, got caught up in the ropes and had a fatal heart attack right next to the catatonic chump.

Two suckers down for the count.

One southpaw headed down to the border.

And me left holding a cute little designer bag and a whole lot of high-interest debt.

***

My grandpa told me that in the Middle Ages, folks thought left-handed people were possessed by the devil. There may be some truth to that. One thing's for certain—nothing good ever comes from trusting a southpaw, especially Benji Jackson.

It's got me thinking that maybe it's time I stop looking for reasons to break Grandpa's rules and start living them instead.

Make my own destiny.

Be my own damn unicorn.

Mr. Louie was a good talker, but I'm a better listener. He taught me everything there is to know about fixing fights, and he introduced me to every major player in Vegas, too—including a right-handed heavyweight with two felony convictions and one serious crush on me named Ricky "The Mexicutioner" Ramirez.

It wasn't hard to get Ricky on board for a little road trip to Ensenada. One way or the other, I'm getting my $50K back. One way is simply appealing to Benji's sense of fairness. The other? Well, that's why The Mexicutioner is along for the ride. It'd be a shame if Ricky had to shatter Benji's high cheekbones. But Benji made his choice, And I've made mine.

After that, I figure I'll pick up where Mr. Louie left off—start calling the shots for a change. I'm done leaving things to fate. Or men. From now on, my primary investment will be in Destineé.

LISA ROBERTSON (on Facebook @LisaPooh23) is a magazine editor and features writer living in the middle of nowhere, Texas. You can find more stories from Lisa at *Writer's Playground* and *Next Tribe*. When she's not writing, Lisa is usually baking or spoiling her grandson (often with things she bakes).

Kings and Elk

Ann Wuehler

Mike bled. His naked body shivered in the chilly air of the Sawtooths. He told himself he was the alpha male here. He was the top predator—king of the jungle, prince of the forest.

The bull elk charged again, crazed by mating lusts.

Mike grunted as the antler tips speared his shoulders and chest but he managed to grab the ears, twist them a bit before the animal backed off. It pawed the ground. Mike's blood dripped from the tines.

He vowed to defeat this bag of meat. If it killed him, let the world weep at his bravery. Let his name be recorded as a name of honor.

Mike ignored the throb of his shoulder as his head filled with the thought of people smiling at him, lowering their eyes when he strode past. He envisioned women, in glittery, slinky gowns, holding their breath as he told the tale of what he had done this day in the wilds.

"Hey!"

A woman rode a palomino between him and his prey The slight wind caught her short black hair, the sun gave it the shine of a crow's feathers. She wore crisp olive-green pants, a pale green shirt tucked into those pants, and a dark green jacket with an Idaho Forestry badge on her left sleeve.

The elk bugled and pawed the earth. Other elk bugled back. Mike throbbed to rejoin the battle, his blood trickling down his bare chest. The need to defeat this chosen foe consumed him. It coursed through him faster than light itself. Nothing would get in his way, not if he remained steadfast and true, trite as that was. Manhood was built on being true to domination and the triumph of will over another. You stood atop the mountain, or you drowned in shit at the base. There was no other way to be.

"Get out of my way," Mike growled.

"I'm having you arrested for trespassing and hunting without a license," the woman replied. "Public indecency. And suicidal. You nutbags, out here trying to battle the local wildlife. Why not a bear? Why is the challenge always an elk? Who thinks of this shit? Stop it!"

This weirdo, with her bitter need to end his journey, began to write in a leather-bound notebook. A forest cop? Why was he always thwarted? Nothing he tried ever came to anything . . . No, that was defeatist thinking.

Life existed to be conquered by those tough enough to handle it. He had shaped his body into a weapon. He had given up brownies and girlfriends. His sister told him he needed therapy. His own dad rolled his eyes and said real men don't need to tell everyone they're real men all the damn time. What did that jackwagon know about being real? None of that mattered now. Nothing mattered but this moment—this moment of facing the utter savagery of nature at its worst.

He stood six four and weighed near two hundred fifty pounds, all of it muscle and protein shakes. The elk had to weigh about eight hundred pounds or more. He caught glimpses of it as it pawed the earth, as it called out. It would sprint away to find cows if he did not engage it in a death match for the ages! His name would be synonymous with courage! The movie about this would break all box office records. *Oh God*, he moaned deep inside his quivering, moist soul, *let it begin, let me conquer.*

The magnificent antagonist would not get away. It would not win because of some lady bureaucrat. She wrote in her notebook, snickering at him. She snickered. Where had she even come from? How could he be trespassing on public lands in a public forest?

The time had come to act.

Mike tried to just dart past her and continue his quest for dominance.

He ran at the palomino, at the irritation of this ridiculous female messing up this pristine world of battle, of flesh against flesh, soaked in the very fluid of life itself. What did she know of war, of clawing up a solid rock face with raw, blistered hands to ascend to the very top of the world? What did she know of conquest and winning?

The elk charged.

It ran right at the horse, at the woman, at him, screaming defiance, screaming like all the devils in hell let loose.

Mike screamed back, ready to die with his hands about that thick furry throat, choking on his chosen enemy's hot, salty blood.

Instead, the woman turned her magnificent horse toward the elk even as she removed her jacket, her pale green shirt pulled free, revealing her fish-white bulgy little belly. She flung the jacket into the buck's face as she flashed by the cervid and it stumbled to a halt, snorting and shaking that antlered head to rid itself of the cloth blinding it so suddenly.

The woman turned her horse and rode it toward Mike, who gaped at such unsportsmanlike conduct.

"Look, you naked, bleeding idiot. Go back to Payette or wherever you're from. Pretend this never happened. No ticket. No sense kicking someone when they're down. I get it. You wanna be king of the mountain or lord of the rings, I can't keep the fantasies straight anymore. You're the fourth guy I've had to save from a bull elk this week alone. Stop it. You wanna bag one? Get a license, wear some clothes, shoot it. Bow hunting! That's manly. Oh for the love of honeydew melons—is that with you?"

He turned to see a naked man, with a balding head and a slight paunch, emerge from the trees to the left. Mike had also walked up that narrow path from where he had camped by Alice Lake. The newbie stopped, jaw falling adrift as he surveyed blood-smeared Mike, the woman on the horse, and the now-pacified, disoriented elk.

The elk shook off the Forestry jacket. The woman turned her horse and chased it off. The big deer bounded off peacefully into the pines and huckleberry bushes. It bounced toward the tree line far, far above

Mike howled at seeing such a worthy foe escape his wrath. His cry rang outward like the screech of a bagpipe, like the roar of a lion denied its zebra prize. The other man howled as well, making a sort of hybrid wolf howl and cat scream.

These two outpourings of anger and rage at being so thwarted were met by a third, a fourth, and yes, a fifth yowling. Three more naked men, ready to battle whatever they must for dominance and success, burst from other directions and the woman began to laugh. She laughed so hard she bent over with her mirth, clinging to the horse so she didn't fall off.

Five men had answered the challenge. Five men out of millions, thought Mike with real pride.

His shoulder ached. The blood had dried to an itchy patina on his goose-bumped skin. Something had bitten his left buttock. He had a cut on the bottom of his right foot. Warrior wounds, battle scars that he could show with pride and integrity.

I dare, he thought. I dare where others cower.

The woman got off her horse to retrieve her jacket. "I thought I'd seen it all, I really had." Up she clambered, back onto her mount, which shook that long mournful head and danced a bit until the woman clamped her knees around the shining ribs and said something into the twitching, swiveling ears. She reached into the back pocket of her pants, took out her phone, and snapped several pictures of Mike and the four other naked men.

"You can't do that," the balding paunchy man whimpered.

"I'll sue your ass, I'll sue it so hard," the one who had long blondish braids and the build of a skinny Viking added, shaking his finger at the woman on the horse.

"You do that, cupcake. And I'll post me some pictures of five stupid men with a death wish. Five naked stupid men with their wieners hanging out. Yee ha and slap my Aunt Fanny, boys! Go have some hot chocolate and calm down." The strange woman chuckled, gave them a smile and a nod, before she left the five to their fate.

The palomino whinnied, the pale gold silk of tail and mane floating in the Idaho mountain air as the woman rode due east, or maybe west., Mike had no sense of direction or purpose after his near-epic battle with the grand bull elk. He was prepared for only one of two outcomes: he would have either won or died with his hands crushing that proud throat.

His dreams had nearly come true, and now it felt like they had been stolen from him. Dreams deferred, however, were not dreams denied, and surely, they would not die so easily.

Dreams? You watched a stupid challenge on You Tube. You didn't even know about this last week, you kangaroo.

His sister's voice had become one of the taunting voices in his head. Mike could not erase her tones from his brain.

One could get a new dream. Or one could still hang onto the old dreams.

"What do we do now?"

Mike turned to the Viking wannabe and he sniffed, his throat closing to a narrow tunnel. Something in him broke at seeing four other men, naked as babies, waiting to be led. Where were the grand men of this age? Where were they? He wished, oh, to be led as well, to be told to go back to his pup tent, pack it up and go home, to Caldwell.

Hot chocolate sounded good.

Payette. As if!

"We find another elk," Mike offered but he did not use words. His lips seemed glued shut. His eyes stung.

"We should hunt down a bear," said the man with black hair and the scar of some awful operation twisting from his misshapen knee to his groin and hip.

"I got hot chocolate," said the paunchy man, eyes on the crushed grasses beneath his feet. "We can, uh, plan. Maybe it counts if we, uh, if we're like, like a pack? We could be a pack. Like wolves!"

"That isn't how it works," the Viking whined, twisting his long blondish braids about his fingers. He had tiny nipples and had shaved all over. "Hot chocolate?"

"I'll try again. And again. Until I kill one or it kills me," Mike wanted to say. He wanted to be the leader of this group. The alpha male! Instead, he nodded and trailed the others. They thumped along like a line of baby ducklings. He wept inside, the laughter of the women echoing in his ears, his eyes on the naked rump of the paunchy, balding man.

I am not a baby duckling, Mike told himself. *The challenge said fight an elk. But . . . what if I took on a bear?*

His mind trembled at such glory that would await surviving that. He'd be somebody. He'd be somebody at last.

ANN WUEHLER (on Facebook @AnnRWuehler) has written six novels—*Aftermath: Boise, Idaho, Remarkable Women of Brokenheart Lane, The House on Clark Boulevard, Oregon Gothic, The Adventures of Grumpy Odin and Sexy Jesus* and *Owyhee Days*. Her stories have appeared in various venues including Brigid Gate's *Crimson Bones* anthology, *Along Harrowed Trails, Penumbric, World of Myth, Whistle Pig, Stygian Lepus,* and others. You can find her online at annwuehler.wordpress.com.

THE LIT. MAG THAT'S LEAVING ITS MARK ON CRIME FICTION.
ROCK AND A HARD PLACE
MAGAZINE
Issues 1-15 available now!
www.rockandahardplacemag.com

MARCH 2025 PROMPT — March is in like a lion and out like a lamb, but this month at **Stone's Throw**, we want to reverse it. Give us meek characters who find their fire by the end of the story. What happens when repression gives way to hedonism and rage? Or maybe your protagonist was already a secret badass, and just needed that nudge to show their true stripes? Maybe they go too far, and have to make sense of what they've done when they come back to their senses? Keep it within the usual **RHP** boundaries.

Be Your Own Boss

AD Schweiss

There's a feeling your voice gives me, like I'm made of iron the way you must be. *I want you to imagine a debt-free life.* The way you say the words, like leading me through gunfire or to the top of a mountain. Every word you say, like a TED Talk on the edge of the world.

The thing about starting a business is that no one tells us what it means to give a hundred percent. For some people it means graduate school or an MBA. But for me—*my* truth—maybe giving one hundred percent means finding your address with an online background check and driving all night to meet you.

I replay one of your Instagram posts over and over: you say the words *I had to spend money to make money.* It's the way your voice slips the heroine mask and you almost sob. In that video you talked about starting a business the way other women talk about unmedicated childbirth. There's a part in the video where the ring light flares the gloss on your lips to an electric white and your eyes mist while you speak like a storm cloud.

I want to lionize *my* sacrifices; I want to have frozen moments when I am knocked down and get up again; I want resilience that other women can drink up for themselves. I want to be an anthem the way you are for me, and the closeness of locked arms and knowing we are all in the same fight.

I bought my first vitamins from you—the second most-expensive package you call 'Fempire'—almost as an afterthought. And then right after that I went out and found the nicest lipstick in CVS. Matching the rose of your lips in my own face, because I never found a better way to hold on to the drive you've given me.

Now I carry your vitamins in my car wherever I go, which you said to do in one of your videos; so heavy they make it hard to brake on the highway. I brought them with me to meet you.

I watched you leave your house just now with a trash bag, padding on your toes, the ground stinging your feet like someone walking on Legos. I know what that feels like—to do mundane things for your family in bare feet—except your ordinary movements are pumped full of grace and my husband looks at my body like a chore. I look at your muscles, like some lean jungle animal built for survival: a predator. And if I had legs like yours, I would feel wild and unexpressed emotions. I just know I would.

I want to leave behind the drudge of my family's garbage, or have those humdrum moments infused with your sense of purpose until my heart beats something high-octane and I can drive away the cold fog of my mornings.

I've been watching you for a while now. *It takes guts to take the first step*. That's what you said in another one of your videos, and I had to watch it three times to find my nerve. But it takes guts to take that *final* step, too—getting too near you feels dirty, like touching an exhibit at a museum and all I wanted to say to you this morning was: *I want the secrets to selling, and to growing my business. I want you to share your spark.*

Because I'd only worked with you through your online video series, I know that I'm not exactly getting the real thing; the *real* you. At home I would think to myself: maybe your essence online is one-hundredth of what it is in real life. Just being in your presence now—standing here with you—I know how true that was; how *right* I was and that means something about the connection we have. I can see in your eyes—your real, in-person eyes—the grit and energy that makes you a source of power for other women. I want to be your right-hand woman and I'm sorry that me saying so is scary to you, but you should have put the phone down when I asked.

You don't need to call the police.

One of the things you always talk about is not surrendering to *No*. You talk in your videos about how, as women, we're made to cheer for so many people from the sidelines: husbands and children and people at work. Your neon-pink lips that form the *ooo* when you ask *What about you* stirred something wild in my guts, and there's a courage in me that caught fire when I heard you tell me not to take no for an answer.

Leaving your garage would absolutely be taking no *for an answer and I am not taking no for an answer and I need you to calm down. Do you even understand how many vitamins I need to sell? My husband says they're going to repossess our truck.*

In my wildest fantasies you were going to say: *I think we have so much to learn from each other.* You promised me '24-hour executive support' when I became one of your Personal Growth Executives and then when you blocked me on Instagram it felt like sitting alone in high school. So now you need to close the garage door because you're being loud which is unprofessional of you. And whether it's fair or not I feel trapped by the memory of the way I told my husband *I have to spend money to make money*, the words dribbling out like water from broken plumbing with no pressure, like I couldn't believe in myself with his eyes on mine, not even for a moment. I have so many questions:

Does your husband ever look at you like you're *less than* him? Who handles the finances in your house? How much did you risk to become your own boss? What was the darkest time? Was it worse than what I'm doing right now?

I wouldn't have to point it at you if you just listened to me.

Are your kids well-behaved? How do you have the time to exercise? Do you feel like you *made it*? I think you do—or you should, if you don't. Your garage is bigger than my whole house.

If we sat down together in an interview, or if you let me inside your home just now and we talked over coffee, I think the questions I would ask you would show you how much our souls are paired together; how we're navigating the same constellation of emotions and we're like sisters on the ocean of our shared hearts.

Do you ever feel like you're on my side of the same ugly mirror, looking at a better woman on the other side who can afford nice salads for lunch, whose kids are good at sports? Do you ever feel bad about your neck? How can I find a diamond in the center of my gut that my husband can't take from me, no matter how I look on the outside?

Where can I sell sixteen hundred bottles of vitamins before the 24th?

There's an itch down the center of my spine just from looking at you, nagging at places I can't dig from outside: I want your phone number, and to get calls from you just to check in. I want us to drop off our kids at the same school at the same time and to go for walks afterward. And even if I had those things—even if I stood on the same peak as you and saw the world from your high country—I think what I want is to pull out everything under my skin so you can fix me from the inside out.

Don't think I won't do it, you bitch.

I came all this way for you.

AD SCHWEISS (on BlueSky @adschw.bsky.social; on Twitter / X @adschweiss) worked as a prosecutor in California for 14 years, with the majority of his time spent handling crimes of intimate partner violence. His short fiction has appeared in **RHP Press**, *Shotgun Honey*, *BULL*, and a few other places. He currently resides in Spokane with his troublesome wife, his troublesome kids, and a well-behaved dog.

At Sixes and Sevens

Brittany Hague

S cottie was determined. He would not spiral, he wouldn't. Yes, he'd found seven grey hairs that morning, but he had also booked his first appearance in years with KIIS FM. And his crystals, which he consulted every morning before digging into his Fruit Loops, were vibrating at a new frequency, confirming that his life was about to change.

But seven grey hairs are not zero. Luckily, he had a cut and dye appointment with Chauncy who was finally back from his natural magik retreat. Scottie stuck his tongue out in the hallway mirror, made the spinning "cuckoo" motion with his middle fingers at each side of his head (his signature move,) and hurried to the salon. He was freaking bursting with optimism.

Chauncy's place on Sunset smelled of the tropics and was gleaming white save for the huge, colorful graffiti mural that covered the salon's back wall, a mural that really meshed with Scottie's whole vibe.

"Miss Cassie will not be covering the cost of this appointment."

The bronzed, elven hairdresser delivered the devastating news as placidly as an ice sculpture. It was hard to tell if Chauncy was heartless to Scottie's predicament or if it was his new cheek and brow work.

Scottie stared into the mischievous eyes of the anamorphic spray paint can in the corner of the mural, but neither answers nor comfort were to be found there either.

"I don't get it, Chauncy. I need my faux hawk, like, today. I have an appearance."

Chauncy raised his long-fingered hands and pranced a few paces back, "Don't kill the messenger, honey. She didn't call and tell you? She certainly left plenty of messages with me."

"I don't know! I've been off the grid, meditating and channeling energies, so I can work on a new song for the event. It's later today. I can't show up like this."

Scottie had been the "wild one" of the minor pop-punk band, At Sixes and Sevens, and his signature look was a bright green faux hawk and a double venom tongue piercing. He still had the titanium barbells, but his hair had gone mousy and flat.

It was Scottie who wrote the lyrics to the band's only hit sixteen years ago; a single that had gone gold just this last year--*Hey, dad, you're nothing but a suburban sheep. You spend and complain, and you whine, and you bleat. Your rules and your laws make me mad. You're nothing but a suburban sheep, dear dad.*

He looked in the mirror. Jowly, pasty, old. *Oh man, I'm the "Suburban Sheep" now,* he thought. He felt like crying.

Miss Cassie was the widow of At Sixes and Sevens' former manager, Richie Barbary. Of the whole band, she had chosen Scottie. Not handsome lead singer Marc, not the guitarist Chris who stood at six foot five, and definitely not the chubby drummer Pete, whose Christmas cards arrived in Scottie's mailbox every year. The wholesome images of Pete and his family on their farm in Vermont, well . . . there was no point denying it. They brought Scottie to tears.

Holidays were a lonely time for him. What did he even have? A one-bedroom rented condo, his monthly massages and manicures, his rare Pez dispenser collection. All paid for by Miss Cassie who only called him a few times a month anymore and when she did, it was just for him to fill an empty seat at Raspoutine or Nobu.

Scottie had keys to her penthouse and everybody—the doormen, the maintenance guys, the pool boys—they all knew him. But not one of them smiled and greeted him as usual that afternoon.

Gerry, who ran the mail room, was the only one to approach. He put his hand on Scottie's shoulder.

"Hey Scottie, you sure you're supposed to be here?"

"Yeah, man I'm exactly where the universe wants me."

"Miss Cassie has a guest," Gerry said, "why don't you head home, and you can text her, come another day."

"I don't mind guests," Scottie said, brushing off the hand and letting the elevator door close on Gerry.

But something about Gerry's furrowed brow gave him pause. He checked his phone. Miss Cassie had indeed left several messages over the past few days, but when he began to play the most recent one "Oh Jesus, sweet cheeks, you can't avoid me forever. I want-" He stopped the recording. She sounded drunk and guilty. No thank you.

He turned his attention to his reflection in the elevator mirror. Unable to afford anything more than a trim with the cash he had on hand, Scottie had resorted to turning his hair green with Halloween spray he found at Ralph's. It looked . . . well, it wasn't exactly what he was going for, but as he slapped the skin under his chin and sucked in his cheeks, he could almost see his old self, if he squinted. *She can't dump me,* he told himself. *She's practically a senior citizen at this point.* The elevator ding announced his arrival.

The penthouse was dark, which was strange, because the north and west walls were windowed. She must have shut and drawn the blinds. Hung over, he assumed. He bent to take off his combat boots, not in the mood for her lecture about the rugs, when he stumbled over something. He fell to one knee and heard a crack. It was Richie's prized Teen Choice Award surfboard. She had moved all her husband's gold and silver records and awards to the condo when he died, as though they were her own achievements. He tried to survey the damage in the dim light. No doubt, she was going to chew his ass for this one, even though it was her fault for leaving it out.

He picked up the board and found that one of the fins was slick, wet.

Gross.

Then he saw it.

Not it. Him.

Fort Noxxx, splayed out on the floor, probably drunk.

Scottie should have known. Before Richie Barbary had died a few years ago, he had signed Noxxx, a young hip hop artist who knew how to market himself on social media. He was a skinny white kid from the South with a slow Georgia drawl and a teardrop tattoo under one eye. He had recently dyed his buzzed hair green.

So was that Miss Cassie's kink? Hadn't she been the one to encourage Scottie's own lime locks?

The last time he'd seen Miss Cassie, a couple weeks ago, she had left Scottie alone with her dog walker at a corner booth in Mother Wolf while she went to the little girl's room. Scottie had been so enthralled with the conversation, apparently most dogs are reincarnated saints, a fact he did not know, that he did not question her when she returned over an hour later nor did he pay too much attention to the fact that once again, Fort Noxxx had shown up where they were eating. The attention the rising star garnered from waitstaff made Scottie jealous, but he was too trusting, he guessed, to suspect anything was going on with Miss Cassie.

Scottie kicked Fort Noxxx in the side, gently, to wake him up. Noxxx didn't move, but a sudden ray of light illuminated his head and the wound that, Scottie now realized, was gushing blood onto Miss Cassie's expensive rug.

The light came from the now-open bedroom door, in the middle of which stood Miss Cassie. She froze. "It wasn't me. I mean, he deserved it . . . what are you doing here, Scottie?"

"Is he freaking dead?"

She was disheveled, in pink sweatpants, high heels, and a tank top. Her eyes looked small. He realized all this time, he'd never seen her without her fake lashes, not even when they made love. Her hair was in a ponytail and thin. It was like looking at a stranger, a murdering stranger, and he dropped the surfboard and stumbled back toward the front door.

"Stop! You, you're jealous. You barged in here; you struck him with the board. I'm sorry sweet cheeks but that's what happened. You did this."

"What? I didn't do anything! Have you gone cray?"

"Who's going to believe you? The dumped boyfriend shows up . . ."

"So, you are dumping me. Is this some kind of joke? Did they bring Punk'd back?"

"I'm going to scream, Scottie." But as she inhaled, Fort Noxxx gurgled, spit, and sat up. The shock made them both scream. "No! You need to be dead," Miss Cassie took one of her stilettos and ran at Fort Noxxx.

Scottie sprang into action. He reached Noxxx first and dragged him to the nearest bathroom, slamming the door behind him on the advancing and angry Miss Cassie.

Through the locked door, she whined. "You gotta help me, Scottie. I don't know what I was saying before. Of course I'm not dumping you. We've had a good thing for a long time. It's that boy, he's got me all mixed up. He's dangerous. He's the one that wanted me to cut you off. You need to finish this, sweet cheeks. Then we'll be together. It was an accident and a woman like me is not made for prison. Can you hear me?"

Scottie took his good luck hoodie, the one he'd worn on the Warped Tour, from his waist and wrapped it around the wound on Fort Noxxx's skull.

Fort Noxxx, cradled in Scottie's arms, looked up at him. "Y'all from another planet? Come to take me to be with grandmama?"

"What?" Scottie looked in the mirror. The spray paint was sweating down his face, turning his forehead green. It was pathetic, he realized, and wouldn't have fooled anyone. He was washed up, a man-child dependent on Miss Cassie but he wasn't sure he was ready to be anything more than that.

How did one kill a man? Scottie had always been a spacy, soulful person, the kind of son that disappoints a dad like his; ex-military, mean, stoic. He glanced around the bathroom. Beating with a plunger? Poison by Le Mer moisturizer? He decided drowning would be easiest. Fort Noxxx could simply bleed out in the water.

Miss Cassie would be grateful, so grateful she would let him move into the penthouse, making their arrangement permanent and real. They could even get married, have children via surrogate. A girl and two boys would be nice. He'd send his own Christmas card, a farm in Vermont, a reindeer sweater, the carefree confident smile of a man whose root chakra was healed, whose abundance had been manifested.

Or maybe he'd call 911. He'd miss his appearance at the fun run that day but would be hailed as a hero for saving Fort Noxxx. Requests for interviews would follow. Not only from KIIS FM, but other local radio stations and television too, maybe even Good Morning America, for which he could sport a new, distinguished silver fox faux hawk.

Indebted to Scottie for saving his life, Fort Noxxx would release a remix of his song, "Bathtub" (featuring Dove Cameron) that could sample "Suburban Sheep." Scottie would even get to play bass and sing on it. What if it turned out to be a hit? What if it was featured in some sort of viral bubble bath commercial or a new Netflix comedy? That could pay enough for a down payment on an apartment. Sure, it might not be west facing and as large as the one Miss Cassie provides, but he could find one with built-in shelves for his crystals and collections, and most importantly, it would be his.

Scottie wasn't a nobody. His choices mattered.

As he held Noxxx closer, the seconds ticked down to deciding his fate. His arms felt sticky and slick and when he looked down, he was dumbfounded. Real blood was darker than it was in the movies. And a body wasn't the same thing as a person. The soul of Fort Noxxx, whose blank eyes were staring blindly up at Scottie, had become one with the universal energy, and Scottie was left holding its shell. He rocked it back and forth, still weighing his options, as if he had any, as a siren's mournful wail drifted closer.

BRITTANY HAGUE (she/her; on Instagram @unluckyyarn) works as a graphic artist and short story writer in Seattle, WA where she lives with her husband, two children, and familiars. Her short stories have appeared in the *Night of the Geminids* and *Monster* (Hidden Fortress Press) anthologies, *Last Girls Club*, *Willows Wept Review*, and *Bog Fancy* and have been featured on the *Kaidankai* and *Short Story Today* podcasts. She is a graduate of film and video at The Rhode Island School of Design. Learn more about her work at https://www.brittanyhague.com/.

MAY 2025 PROMPT — The saying goes that necessity is the mother of invention, and this month, in honor of Mother's Day, we want your stories focused on Mama Bears backed into a corner. What will they do to protect their cubs? How do they invent a justification for crossing the uncrossable line? And was it all worth it? Remember, the tagline for **Rock and a Hard Place** is "bad decisions and desperate people."

Goodbye Tommy

Tammy Blakley

I swear I told Darlene over and over again not to get messed up with that Jenkins boy, Tommy. That whole family wasn't nothing but no good. Hell, what'd ya expect from that clan. Old Man Jenkins had been in prison for the last fifteen years for killing that schoolteacher that failed Tommy in fifth grade for setting the gym on fire. Little fucker was twelve years old and already an arsonist.

Darlene had a chance to make something of herself. She'd always been a good student, bringing home mostly As and Bs. Told me once she wanted to be a nurse so she could help people. This was after she watched her daddy die from emphysema. I'm surprised we all didn't die as much as he smoked. Maybe that's what messed her up.

Senior year about three months before graduation, Darlene told me she was gonna marry Tommy. He gave her some dime store ring and an empty promise of getting her out of this one-horse town.

I laughed when she said all this. "Baby, he don't even have a job."

"Mama, you don't know! You just don't know! He loves me and I love him. We'll show you."

A week later she'd dropped out of school and run off to the courthouse with Tommy. Twenty bucks later, the justice of the peace pronounced them man and wife. They spent their wedding night in Tommy's twenty-year-old pickup truck because he didn't even have enough money to get a thirty-dollar room at the flophouse motel out by the interstate.

I spent the next week in a daze, not eating or sleeping, wondering what I'd done so wrong to Darlene to send her off to this two-bit jackass. She finally called me and said Tommy found them a place to live. The yard manager at the sawmill had an old tool shed he'd rent to them for fifty bucks a month. It had electricity and running water but no bathroom. A port-a-potty the mill workers used sat close by.

"Honey, you can come home. Your room's still like you left it."

"Mama, I'm a married woman now. I belong here with my husband. It's gonna be alright. Tommy's saving money so we can get a better place."

Tuesday of the next week I went to get my hair done at Maxine's. She'd done my hair for as long as I'd lived here and was my best friend. We'd been through a lot together. Most of it we had to keep secret because Maxine's husband was a deputy. When I walked in, she had a look on her face.

"There you are. Where've you been? Why aren't you answering your phone?" Maxine grabbed my arms.

"What are you going on about?" I'd known Maxine for a long time and never seen her so out of sorts.

"It's Darlene. Jimmy's been looking for you. He got called out to that shed Darlene and Tommy live in, workers passing by heard screaming and called dispatch. When he got there, Darlene was all beat up. Black eye, busted lip. Tommy was holding onto her and telling her it'd all be ok. Told Jimmy that she tripped and fell and hit her face on the table. He said, 'Ain't that right, Babe?' and she nodded. Said she's clumsy and fell."

Bile rose in my throat as I thought of what Tommy did to her. "Where is she? Is she okay?"

"Paramedics went out there and patched her up, but couldn't nobody ever get her to admit he'd touched her so there was nothing Jimmy could do."

"Goddammit, I knew this was gonna happen. Told her not to get messed up with that family."

Maxine put a hand on my shoulder. "Honey, there's more. They took her to the hospital anyway because she was . . . bleeding."

My breath caught in my throat. "She's pregnant?"

Maxine nodded.

The panic I felt gave way to red hot rage.

"We've got to go." I stormed to the door.

"Right behind you." Maxine took off her apron, grabbed her purse and locked the front door, flipping the sign over to Closed.

We got to the county hospital and found Darlene's room. She was propped up in the bed with an IV hanging out of her arm and a tube up her nose. Her eyes were closed, one of them swollen shut. Darlene looked like a paper doll, lying there, crumbled, just another thing for Tommy to burn.

A nurse was taking her vitals and writing them down on a clipboard.

"What did that mother fucker do to her?" I ran to Darlene's side, grabbing one of her hands and brushing the hair back off her forehead.

"Hi, I'm Bethany. I'm her nurse. Are you her mother?" Bethany set the clipboard down and gave me one of those smiles that weren't the happy kind but the I'm so sorry kind.

"Yes, how is she? Is she gonna be okay?" Seeing her like that, imagining that son of a bitch doing this to her set my blood boiling. I could hear Maxine and the nurse talking but their words didn't register. All I could focus on was my broken baby girl and the fact that Tommy still burned everything he touched.

"Why don't we come sit over here and I'll get her doctor to come talk to you?" She guided me toward a hard plastic chair by the window. "I'll be right back."

Maxine came up beside me, rubbing my back. "She's gonna be okay."

Inside, I felt my pulse drumming through my head like a sledge-hammer. I clenched my fists so hard both palms bled from my finger-nails.

"Hi, Mrs. Sanders, I'm Doctor Wilson." He pulled another chair over in front of me and sat down. "Your daughter is stable now, but she's not out of the woods. I'm afraid she suffered some internal bleed-ing. We think we have that taken care of, but we are still monitoring her. The next twenty-four hours are critical. I'm afraid we couldn't save the baby."

Nodding, I bit my lip and glanced over at Darlene. Three weeks until her birthday. Nineteen. I remembered all the sleepless nights when she was a baby, her first steps, the skinned knees, fevers, sore throats, joy at Christmas, heartbreak at not getting invited to Sarah's birthday party, the first time she drove off by herself. I remembered eighteen other birthdays, trying to find the right gift, but I already knew what she was getting this year.

"Thank you, Doctor. I need to take care of something, then I'll be back. You make sure she's okay. She's got a birthday coming up." I stood.

"I'll do everything I can for your daughter." He shook my hand on his way out.

I went over to Darlene's bed. "I'll be back, Baby Girl." I bent down and kissed her forehead. "Mama's got this."

Maxine followed me out. We were in her car before either of us spoke. She stuck a cigarette between her lips and lit up.

"Where to?"

"The hardware store." An eerie calm settled over me as I watched the red-hot end of her cigarette glowing when she inhaled.

I made my purchases and loaded them in the trunk of Maxine's car. The sawmill was only a mile away. Lunchtime. All the workers would be on break at the diner just up the road.

Maxine parked behind a stack of logs. I could hear Tommy snoring through the screened window as we got out and crept up to the shed. Maxine held out her hand. I took it and squeezed.

"This time's for Darlene."

It always amazed me at how fast paint thinner got an inferno going. A couple gallons, less than ten bucks, splashed outside that old wooden shed full of paint cans and solvents.

Flames shot up faster than the school gym did back when Tommy set it on fire.

And the best part? I could hear Tommy screaming over the roar of the fire.

"You play with matches, Tommy . . ." Maxine and I watched, waiting for his screams to stop before getting back in the car. I felt the heat through the passenger side window as the shed collapsed. Fire cleanses, leaving nothing in its wake.

"Take me back to the hospital, Maxine."

TAMMY BLAKLEY (on Bluesky @tammywritesbooks.bsky.social; on Twitter / X @tammy_blakley) lives in the Pacific Northwest where she spends her days writing mysteries or staring out the window at her gorgeous view of Mt. Baker. She completed her first manuscript with no formal training and a total lack of adult supervision. She enjoys the support of her amazing husband who, so far, hasn't recommended medication. She has previously published stories in *Punk Noir Magazine* and *Urban Pigs Magazine*.

JUNE 2025 PROMPT – Happy Pride Month! **Rock and a Hard Place Press** is a proud ally of the LGBTQ+ community, and this month, we want stories where the pride rainbow isn't quite as bright. Queer characters (and queer people, for that matter) put up with enough bullshit from homophobes and transphobes, and this month we want noir tales where they turn the tables on the haters in fabulous and brutal ways.

Double Feature

Jenn Hooker

I didn't realize I was bleeding until I saw the abstract red splatters on the brick beneath me. The adrenaline coursing through my veins kept me from feeling anything, tasting anything, hearing anything. My senses were completely dulled. My mind, though . . . my mind was as sharp as a tack.

Unfortunately, that sharp mind of mine was in defense mode. The muscles in my abdomen contracted, my arms flew up to my head, and I pulled into the fetal position as blows rained down on my head. Kicks connected with my spine and legs, and my sharp mind began praying to a god I didn't really believe in that I would survive the next five minutes.

"Fat dyke bitch," the guy spat at me, and landed one more hit before his friend pulled him away.

"Come on, Knucks, that's enough."

Their thick-soled black boots smacked on the brickwork as they walked away.

I laid there for what seemed like an eternity before trying to get up, the harsh yellow light above the back door to the theater flickering. As my adrenaline faded, the pain started to seep in and I knew if I didn't get myself into my car quickly, I wouldn't be able to get up at all.

***

Back home, I crashed through the door of my apartment and Cherry—my dear, sweet Cherry—didn't panic or scream or cry, just collected the alcohol and gauze from our emergency kit and tended to me like my own private nurse.

I looked up at her through my swollen eyes, at her beautiful, smooth skin and rich, auburn hair, and lifted a pain-ridden hand to brush a curl from her face.

"What happened this time?" she asked, as plainly as asking if I wanted meatloaf or spaghetti for dinner.

"I stepped out for a smoke behind that queer theater on Fourth Street—they were screening *Rope* again—and they were already in the alley. Probably waiting for one of us to come out so they could get a few licks in. Guess I got lucky. Don't worry, though, I have a plan."

"Is that so?" She dabbed an alcohol-soaked cotton ball against the gash on my forehead. It stung like hell.

"Yeah, I'm not going to let those boot-licking fascist fucks win. I *can't*." Cherry locked eyes with me, pity and concern writ large on her face.

"Baby," she cooed at me, "you can't just mow 'em down with your car or jump 'em in an alley. You're lucky all they did this time was give you a couple scratches and bruises."

Her ability to minimize my injuries was impressive, but not unprecedented. Nothing was broken this time, sure, but I was going to have a hell of a time wiping my own ass for the next week.

"I can't keep doing this," she said so quietly that, at first, I wasn't sure I had heard her correctly. "You've come home like this four times over the last six months. As soon as you can stand upright, you're out there picking fights."

"Sometimes the fights pick me," I mumbled.

Her voice grew sterner with each word, her confidence gaining steam. "I'm afraid every time you leave the house that one day I'm going to get a call to come ID your body."

Cherry had only ever been my support, my rock, my best friend, my lover. She hardly ever asked me for anything and this one time—this one time she asked me for something—it was something so massive I couldn't say no.

But I had to.

"Cherry, you know I have to do this, right? It's not just for us; it's for the community. Every time they attack one of us, it emboldens them."

A tear spilled down the plump curve of her cheek and she looked away from me, tossing the soiled cotton ball onto the table. She stood up, the springs of the couch bouncing back and rocking me in a way that jostled my aching ribs.

"I'm going to stay with my mom for a while," she muttered as she slipped into our bedroom and shut the door behind her, leaving me there in silence.

***

Cherry was gone when I woke up. I didn't know if for now or for good. For a week I stumbled around the apartment, struggling to make myself a sandwich let alone bathe or work. In her absence I obsessed over my plan, going over each step in detail, four, five, six times. Maybe if I was successful Cherry would come back. Of course, if it didn't go as I hoped it would, there wouldn't be anyone to pick my body up off the asphalt.

When the bruises on my body had turned a disgusting yellow-green color and I could stand up straight for more than ten minutes, I knew it was time. I drove back to the alley behind the movie theater and parked around the corner and out of sight.

Making sure no one was on this side of the building, I set the scene: a length of pipe nestled behind an errant pile of trash bags of stale popcorn, a container full of gasoline tucked behind the grungy dumpster, and a pair of brass knuckles, the kind with the rainbow oil slick finish, resting comfortingly in the palm of my hand. I pulled out the burner phone I'd picked up, then dialed 911.

"911, what's your emergency?" a nasally voice asked.

I tightened the vocal cords in my throat, making my voice as high as I could, drawing on improv classes from long ago. "Please help me, there are men chasing me and I'm hiding in the alley behind Bergman's Theater. Hurry, please!"

I hung up, hoping against hope that this would work. I slipped the phone back into my pocket, tightened my grip on the brass knuckles, and curled into the fetal position in the middle of the alley.

Within a minute I heard sirens blaring. I saw, down the alley, a cop car pull across the entrance, the alley itself being too narrow to drive down. Two figures got out and, as they approached, I saw it was "Knucks" and his partner. Perfect.

I tucked my head more, obscuring my identity until they were right on top of me.

"Ma'am, are you okay? We got a call about someone being chased."

I lay still, doing my best opossum impression, trying not to let my anxiety and, dare I say, excitement, spring the trap too early.

"Check to see if she's breathing," one of them said. I felt a presence come over my body, cautiously.

That's when I struck.

I lashed out with the knuckles as fast as my body would let me and landed a blow directly on the first cop's nose. He shrieked and stumbled back, knocking into the dumpster and falling over onto his side, grabbing at his face as blood started pouring out of his nose.

"What the fuck?!" said Knucks, standing a few feet away. From the ground I saw him stumble backwards, his hand moving towards his holster.

I jumped up, tackling him before he could unclip his sidearm. My shoulder made contact with his chest and we both went down, our limbs becoming tangled in the process. His bulky body trapped my arm against the ground and I could feel the old brick scraping against the skin on my hand. Although my angle was awkward, I punched at the officer, hitting him first across the head, my fist glancing off his short-cropped hair, but the second one landed directly in his throat. His face turned red and he wheezed, clutching at his neck.

I knew my time was limited, lest one of them call for backup. Ripping my arm out from under him, I unclipped the holster and pulled the gun out, tossing it aimlessly down the alley. I moved over to the cop with the bloody nose, grabbing the hidden pipe along the way. He scrambled to get up, his hands and uniform shiny with blood. At that moment I couldn't help but think it was the same shade of red as Cherry's lipstick. With all the strength I could muster, I brought the pipe down on his head.

There was a loud crack. His body went limp.

I turned my attention back to Knucks, who was still clutching at his throat, trying to shout at me and coming up mute. Pipe in one hand, I grabbed the container of gasoline in the other and approached him. He scrambled backwards, kicking at the brick to get purchase and hasten his movement.

"How does it feel to be voiceless, prick?" I asked, and swung the pipe at his leg, connecting with his kneecap in a sickening crunch. He released a screech that reminded me of a wounded animal.

While he writhed in pain, clutching his knee close to his body, I ripped the walkie off his shoulder for good measure and began splashing the gasoline over him. His hand shot up, the milky white palm a silent plea to stop. I shook the jug, each heave pouring out a gush of pungent gasoline.

"Please" he croaked, "Stop. I have kids."

I retrieved a Zippo from my pocket. "Kids, huh? At least you've got good life insurance." I flicked the lighter, the tiny blue-orange flame dancing. A trickle of liquid slid down his cheek and once again I thought of Cherry.

My beautiful, sweet Cherry.

Her bouncy curls. The slight upturn of the curve of her lips. The tear that slid down her supple cheek the other night. Her deep, sultry voice whispering, "I can't keep doing this."

Was this asshole worth it? If I lit this guy up like a fireworks display, wouldn't there be a hundred more like him waiting in the wings? Could I immolate half the police department and get away with it?

And if I let him go, would my Cherry come back to me?

Knucks peered at me wide-eyed through his splayed fingers, waiting. The lighter grew warm in my hand. I took a deep breath, and decided.

JENN HOOKER (she/her; on Instagram @thejennhooker) is an unapologetically queer crime writer from the San Francisco Bay Area. When she's not hatching new schemes or actively writing, she's spending time with her family, tending to her yard, or curled up with a good book.

JULY 2025 PROMPT — School's out for summer, and this month at the **Throw**, we want stories of junior rocketeers discovering the darker side of summer break. We're looking for noir coming-of-age tales, set against the backdrop of freedom afforded by summer recess. Keep it dark, keep it mean, but don't glorify violence committed against children . . . it's got to be in service to the story.

For Laura

Gabriela Stiteler

The last time I went swimming in Lake Kezar was the summer I turned fourteen. It was the first weekend in June and the lake was entirely still. Other than Mark, there was nobody around to tell us what to do. I brought a bag of sour cherries from the cabin's kitchen, and you brought a case of cheap beer and a pack of cigarettes. We laid the bounty next to our towels and jumped into the water, fully submerged our heads, shocking our systems. When we surfaced, we gasped and then giggled, our teeth chattering, our lips tinted blue.

It was too soon in the season, but these early, secret swims were our tradition.

We retreated to our towels and settled into our routine, drinking and smoking and listening ironically to an AM station that was mostly static. With a certain amount of ambivalence, you took off the top of your suit and stared at me, as if daring me to do the same.

"I don't want lines," you were saying, your eyes hidden behind a pair of sunglasses that would have looked awful on anybody else, a cigarette hanging from your mouth, your hair halfway down your back, streaming water in rivulets.

When we were younger, you'd go into stores with no shoes and pick grapes off the bunches and eat them unapologetically, daring employees to kick you out. You'd stare down Mr. Cashone when he confronted you about the length of your uniform skirt. You'd go into the bathroom and roll it up more. That year, you'd been suspended twice for picking fights. Lately, there was a harder edge to your testing.

Sometimes I knew you better than I knew myself. Sometimes I didn't know you at all.

"Aren't you worried Mark will see?" I asked.

Mark. Your stepfather. To whom much was owed. Who brought us out to the lake for long weekends, who took us on kayaks and let us drink beer and played songs on an acoustic guitar he kept on a stand in a corner of the living room, pausing long enough to tell us stories about when he was younger and wilder, tiptoeing into adulthood with us. "I saw some crazy shit," he'd say, leaving it there, our minds twisting over the many possibilities.

It seemed strange that Mark married your mom, who was careful not to make too much noise or take up too much space. Who spent a lot of time crying in her room with the door closed and the television turned up while we pretended not to hear.

Who didn't stand a chance against you.

But then, no one did. Not really.

You shrugged, leaned back on your towel, and picked up a book by some French theologian about forgiveness. Your quick, indifferent shrugs bordered on casual cruelty. Something that, until recently, you had kept for everyone else. Sitting on the other side of it stung.

"Do you believe in this shit?" you asked. "Victimization and anger and learning to let God's love in?"

"Sure," I said. "Mostly."

"You forgive your father?" You asked and lit another cigarette. I cracked another beer even though I didn't like the way it tasted and debated saying there was nothing to forgive. But it would have been a lie and I was trying very hard to be a good person and some piece of goodness meant telling the truth.

"Mostly," I said again.

You let the subject dangle and drop.

The sun came out. I dozed off. When I woke, the sky was pink and you were standing at the edge of the dock with Mark. There was something about how you held your body, something about his response, that I didn't understand. Not then, anyways.

I turned away, embarrassed.

***

That night, it poured. We snuck into the neighbor's screened gazebo. String lights flickered and somebody was playing the piano with the windows open, the water throwing the sound in unexpected ways.

"It's beautiful here," I said, grasping for something.

"Sure," you said.

"I almost don't want to go back."

You didn't say anything.

"Maybe we can come in a few weeks? Or again at the end of the summer?" I tried again, suddenly desperate to draw you out.

You shrugged one of those tight, indifferent shrugs and said, "Jesus. Stop trying so hard."

"I'm not trying," I said, my voice pitching to a whine.

"Sure," you said. And shrugged again.

And instead of thinking about how you were there for me when my dad died, or how you taught me to ride the trails behind our houses when my mother couldn't get herself out of bed for sadness, or how you punched Cassie Sullivan in the face in the locker room after we lost the state championship when she said some shit about me in front of the rest of the team, I was thinking about the distance that was stretching between us. Instead of letting my disappointment wash over me, like a wave, the way Sister Catherine taught me in sixth grade when I was so sick from the sort of anger that comes with a grief so strong I didn't know myself, I said things to you that I don't remember, even still, when I try.

And then I left. Walked out into the rain with you sitting there staring after me, saying nothing.

It was Mark who eventually found me. Who stopped the car and picked me up a mile down the road. I got in mostly because my anger had burned off, leaving me tired and wet and embarrassed.

"What did she say to make you so upset?" he'd asked. I almost didn't hear the question over the rain and the wipers and the sound of my breathing, which was hard and heavy. Around us the windows fogged and the hair on my arms stood on end.

He felt too close.

"I want to go home," I said.

He was quiet for a minute, his hands gripping the wheel, his face stony and solemn. And then he shook his head quickly and smiled. It was as tight and insincere as your shrugs. "Of course," he said, shifting the car into drive and turning back to the camp. "First thing tomorrow, though. After the rain stops."

***

When I walked into the cabin, you were in your room, the door closed, music playing.

Mark sat on the couch and I went to my room without brushing my teeth or showering. I locked the door and removed my wet clothes and packed my bag. Even then, I wasn't sure who I was trying to keep out.

In the middle of the night, I could hear you fighting with him. About what, I don't know.

***

I dreamt about when we were little and you would come to my house in rain boots and your swimming suit with stick-on earrings and chipped blue nail polish, your hair in one long braid down your back. I dreamt that this little version of you took my father's hunting knife, the one he kept in the shed, that he used for field dressing, and sat under the white pine tree. You ran the blade across your palm and held it up to me, smiling.

***

The next morning, I woke to absolute quiet. The sliding door was open and you were sitting at the edge of the dock, the sun cresting over the tops of the trees, your back to me, your shoulders hunched.

Instead of leaving, which I had promised myself I would do, I went to you.

You were staring at the lake. At Mark's body. Face-down, caught in lily pads at the edge of the shore.

I don't know how long I stood there, staring. Waiting for something to happen. When it didn't, I went back to the house and called for help. Then, I sat next to you in the quiet, listening as the birds started back up, saying nothing.

For this, and so much more, I am sorry.

GABRIELA STITELER (on Instagram @gabrielastiteler) is a writer based in Portland, Maine. Her writing has been published in *Ellery Queen Mystery Magazine*, *Alfred Hitchcock Mystery Magazine*, *The Best of New England Crime Writing*, *Dark Waters Anthology*, *Shotgun Honey Presents: At the Edge of Darkness*, and ***Rock and a Hard Place***. Gabi is active in and appreciative of the New England crime writing community. Lately, she's been thinking about the role of silence in story-telling and redemptive character arcs.

AUGUST 2025 PROMPT – We recognize National Women's Equality Day on August 26, commemorating the adoption of the 19th Amendment in 1920, which granted women the right to vote. This month, we want women-led stories and female-identifying protagonists. The sisters are doin' it for themselves, but when you're on the receiving end of a **Stone's Throw**, that's not always the safest place to be.

#emotionallaborday

Autumn Harrison

Growing up in The Family, we did not do holidays, or birthdays, but that's not the point of this story.

The point of this story is family—lower case f. When I had my own family, it took me a while to figure out what was expected at the holidays. Once, my sweet little girl had to remind me that the Easter Bunny brought baskets filled with chocolate eggs and marshmallow chicks. That one still confuses me. What does the Easter Bunny have to do with the torture-killing of a 2,000-year-old peace and love guru? Birthdays were easier: bake a cake, make a meal, and invite everyone.

I'd learned kitchen magic in The Family and could stretch a meal intended for ten into a meal that could feed however many people came to listen to Daddy Charlie preach and riff on his own brand of peace and love. No one was ever turned away, even if they should have been.

My brother's birthday is August 31st, and I've turned it into a yearly open house cookout. Some years, that has meant I was cooking for an ex-husband or two, and a handful of stray kids, and our favorite crossing guard grandma, and my brother's EMT crew, looking for post-shift beers at 8 a.m.. This year was slated to be small: Tabitha, home from college, Junior, my brother, Gavin, my partner, and Karen, his wife.

Yeah, the wife was a problem, five years separated, five years in mediation. First it was the custom detailing business they ran together, then it was the house, and now just the car he had inherited from his father. Gavin, ever the optimist, left the title out on the counter.

I had been working that kitchen magic, ribs in the smoker, cake tiers cooling on a rack, and a hibiscus sun tea brewing on the windowsill, when the familiar growl of the convertible 1962 Mercedes SL pulled into the driveway, gave a shudder, and died.

I pulled a baggy of unripe elderberries from the refrigerator and put them on the countertop. Did I know they were poisonous? I did. Experience had taught me that a little bit of the raw juice would keep an unwelcome guest in the bathroom all day, but a lot would send them to the hospital.

Karen breezed in the backdoor, empty-handed, just like every year, not so much as a smudge stick or a bottle of kombucha. Only this year she brought along Aslan, her new thirty-something yoga instructor boyfriend. A hugger.

"Hope you're cool with me joining?" Aslan asked me, mid-embrace. He was tall, lean, and dressed in an emerald green athleisure outfit: mesh anorak, capri yoga pants, and no underwear—a fact that was impossible not to notice.

"Gloria doesn't mind. She lives for this." Karen answered for me, with a crinkle of her nose.

"Right, why would I?" I replied through my best Get-Along-Gloria smile.

"Hi Karen." Tabitha said. She was wearing cut off jean shorts, a cropped t-shirt that exposed her midriff, and her favorite stompy boots. She was going through a goth moment.

Out of the corner of my eye, I clocked the look Aslan gave to my girl's curvy, compact figure.

Karen had seen it too and tutted, while looking Tabitha up and down, "You've lost those freshman fifteen, thank god."

"Must be all the beer and ramen." Tabitha said and turned to me, "Can I help?"

"Oh yes, Gloria, would you like some help?" Karen chimed in as she and Aslan posed at the back door.

I wondered what she would do if I said yes.

"No, thank you. Go play." I waved my hand out at Gavin and Junior who were throwing a frisbee in the backyard.

"Don't forget to baste both sides of the tofu. Last time it was a little dry." Karen flipped her silk scarf over her shoulder and followed Aslan and Tabitha out the door.

Gavin blamed Karen's spitefulness on their marriage being childless. The phrase he used was 'she has an inhospitable womb.' I think he is a good man, but I might be spiteful too, if I'd heard my uterus described that way.

I picked up the baggie of elderberries and slipped them into the pocket of my new #emotionallaborday apron, a present from Tabitha.

I took a break to restock the cooler on the back deck and could feel Aslan eye-balling the cans of beer.

"Thirsty?" I asked. He licked his lips but shook his head.

Karen said, "No thank you. Alcohol, like sugar, and sex numb the spiritual core."

"My spiritual core is dying for some numbing." Gavin chimed in with a smile and a wink for me.

"Dying is right." Karen said, pointedly staring at Gavin's dad bod belly.

He shrugged.

I was pleased that no one was rising to the bait this year. Turns out I was worried about the wrong thing.

An hour later, I was crouched near the bottom shelves of the kitchen hutch, looking for corn on the cob skewers.

"Mama?" Tabitha's pretty baby doll face was blotchy with high red spots, and streaked with black eyeliner. She was barely holding it together.

I stood up and put my hands on her upper arms.

"He put his tongue in my mouth." The words came out in a violent whispered rush.

"Wait. What?"

"Aslan. He followed me into the powder room. Then he pressed me up against the bathroom sink, said I had a beautiful aura, and put his tongue in my mouth." Her face was filled with confusion and disgust.

My vision shrank to a pin hole, and my grip tightened on her arms. I sucked in a breath and felt it get stuck in my chest.

Greasy trick. I had let him into my home, and he had assaulted my child. Hot prickling rage crawled up my spine and across my scalp. I was going to hurt him.

Tabitha let out a whimper. My hands were clenched into her upper arms. I released my grip and pulled her into a hug.

Her words came out between sucked in gasps, "I pushed him away and tried to leave but he was blocking the door. He scared me but I remembered what Uncle Junior always says and I kneed him in the nuts."

I sat her at the kitchen island and ran a tea towel under the cold-water tap. I held the cool cloth to her brow, watched as she got her breathing under control, and wondered where I had last seen my switchblade.

Then I remembered that Get-Along-Gloria doesn't use a switchblade, and said, "We have to tell Gavin."

Tabitha shook her face away from me, and said, "She'll make a scene."

"Tabitha, you can do it." I fought the urge to grab her by the arms.

Tabitha shook her head again, harder, and said, "No. It's not worth it. I can get along for Junior's Birthday, for Gavin, for the family."

Before I could think of what to say to her, she picked up the placemats and the corn skewers and moved out to the screened-in porch where the table was set up.

My stomach churned with soured rage, and without realizing it, I was rummaging through the drawer that held birthday candles and fast-food condiments, and under the takeout menus, my switchblade. I slipped it into the pocket of my apron.

Everyone has the one dish that makes them feel like a part of a family. There were fried zucchini flowers for Gavin, a citrus salad for Tabitha, and a three-layer chocolate cake for Junior. I took my time juicing the elderberries and adding it to the hibiscus sun tea for Aslan and Karen.

"Are you holding up?" Gavin asked as he came into the kitchen to refill bowls of chips.

"I am. You?" I avoided eye contact and kept my hands busy. I wished that I knew for sure how he would react to hearing that Aslan, Karen's guest, had assaulted my child.

"Just one day, right?"

I nodded and followed him out to the patio, where I served Aslan and Karen glasses of tea, reassuring them that they were alcohol free.

I caught Junior's eye and gestured him toward the kitchen.

"Listen, that greasy trick cornered Tabitha. Stuck his tongue in her mouth."

Junior is normally full of energy and charm, but he can turn on a dime, if need be. He set a newly opened beer down, untasted.

"Keep him here." Junior turned to the back door.

"Hold up, where are you going?"

He looked back at me. "I got my cross-bow in the truck."

"Tabitha asked me not to. She wants to keep the peace, for Gavin."

"Did you macro dose mushrooms this morning? Gavin does not want that."

I held up my hand, "Tabitha needs to know her choices are respected."

"Nope. She needs to know there is only one way to handle greasy tricks. Who is she going to be out in the world, a rabbit or a fox?"

He knew that would get my attention. We had learned a lot the year they arrested all the adults in The Family. Hitchhiking cross country at seventeen with my six-year-old brother in tow, I had a switchblade and a smile, and everyone got a choice.

"Not the crossbow and don't drink the hibiscus tea."

Junior rolled his eyes at me. "You can't fix this problem by giving him diarrhea."

I shrugged and sent Junior back outside with strict instructions not to pick a fight. Out on the sun porch, I sat Tabitha down next to me. "Baby, do you think he has ever assaulted another girl?"

Tabitha's eyes flicked up at me, then down to her hands. But she nodded.

"Do you think he should get away with it?"

She shook her head.

"I am asking you to tell Gavin." I paused, we both needed to know. "If you're worried that keeping the peace is more important to him, let's find out."

She locked eyes with me and I was relieved to recognize the heat of her anger.

"Ok, Mama."

I called Gavin away from the grill and left him alone with Tabitha.

I put the finishing touches on Junior's cake.

Tabitha came back into the kitchen, her face set in determination. Gavin rounded the countertop and kissed me.

"If she tries to defend him, she can keep that car, I don't care."

If she tries to defend him, she will have more than the car to worry about, I thought as I sent Gavin and Tabitha back outside.

I called Karen into the kitchen. She cut me off before I had even gotten to Aslan's 'beautiful aura' line.

She pointed a finger at me. "Really Gloria, this is your fault. You should have told Tabitha that dressing like a slut would get her in trouble."

"Karen, you have a choice. You can be a decent human being and earn a place at my table or you can defend that greasy trick."

She chose wrong.

I reached out and grabbed the ends of her silk scarf, pulling her to me as I slipped the switch blade from my apron pocket and held it between us. I flipped the lever up and felt the satisfying snick of the spring-loaded blade opening.

Karen let out a whistling gasp as I dragged her closer to me and put the tip of the blade to the soft, thin skin under her left eye. She squeezed her eyes closed. There were beads of sweat trapped in the fine bleached hairs above her upper lip.

"You are going to sign the Mercedes title over to my man and then you are going to listen to Tabitha."

I moved my blade to her ribs and gave her a poke, just a little one. I watched her face sag and age, as she signed the back of the title. She looked like a balloon found two weeks after the party. The feeling of control was delicious.

Junior watched me maneuver Karen into the doorway, my knife hidden from view. He nodded to Gavin, who stood up and addressed Aslan, "Tabitha has something to say to you."

Tabitha's face broke out in new red blotches, but she said, "You are a pig. I would never kiss you willingly, ever. What you did was wrong."

"What? Come on, I was just being friendly." Aslan's eyelids were at a languid half-mast.

Gavin crossed the patio in two easy strides and smacked Aslan across the face.

"You are not welcome here." He reached down and picked Aslan up by the collar. The younger man began windmilling his arms until Junior reached over and grabbed a hank of his hair. Together, they frog-marched him out the garden gate.

I poked Karen again, "Start walking, maybe you can hitch a ride."

The rest of the hibiscus tea went down the drain. When the ribs were ready, I took off my #emotionallaborday apron and stowed it next to the takeout menus and my switchblade. I called my family to the table.

Raised in New Orleans and Portland, OR, **AUTUMN HAR-RISON** (on Instagram @autumnharrisonwrites) is a writer living on the edge of Washington, DC with her two darling daughters, and her boyfriend, the race car driver. A former baker, bartender, and band booker she is a fan of crispy cookies, perfect Manhattans, and live music. She longs for the next stage of her life when she can fill her days with motorcycling, knitting, and writing about imperfect people living imperfect lives.

"Raw, brutal, tender, tragic—these are fifteen stories of people smashed flat by the Invisible Fist, people flailing and fighting against the huge and hidden violence at the center of our world. This is crime fiction that matters, crime fiction that is ready to face what comes next."

— Jordan Harper, author of *She Rides Shotgun* and *Everybody Knows*

ON FIRE AND UNDER WATER

A CLIMATE CHANGE CRIME FICTION ANTHOLOGY

Our world is changing dramatically before our eyes.

Those who did the least to cause this crisis will suffer the most from its consequences.

In *On Fire and Under Water*, a crime fiction anthology from Rock and a Hard Place Press, we explore the intersection of climate change and crime, through the lens of fifteen short stories from some of today's best crime fiction writers. Edited by Anthony Award-winning author Curtis Ippolito and the editorial team at RHP Press, the stories contained within this anthology peel back the curtain on the ways in which climate change impacts real people in their most desperate hour.

Some say the world will end in fire. Some say flood. In *On Fire and Under Water*, you get both.

ON SALE NOW, WHEREVER BOOKS ARE SOLD

rockandahardplacemag.com/on-fire-and-under-water

SEPTEMBER 2025 PROMPT – September is smack dab in the middle of Atlantic hurricane season, and the planet is actively trying to kill us all. This month for *Stone's Throw*, give us stories of the Earth in revolt. Hundred year storms every other month. Flash flooding. Tornados. Fire-nados. Bee-nados. Shark-nados. How do your characters cope? And do some of them see opportunity in the face of disaster?

Fire Season

S. B. Nolen

Each year, fire season starts a little earlier on the dry side of the Cascade Range. It's only June, but the dim mountains are already half-hidden by yellow haze; fires that have smoldered deep in the forest duff are breaking out.

Lena sits at the worn kitchen table, alone, watching the sweat on her arms evaporate almost before it appears. The dishes are done and put away, the cast-iron pan back in its place on the stove. Scrubbed with salt and carefully dried to prevent rust. Just as Mark likes it.

She wonders where he is now, the way a pocket mouse listens, immobile, for the silence of an owl.

The little house out in the high desert east of Bend had been Mark's idea, back when he'd lured her away from the rain, from the cold gray winters with promises of year-round sunshine. A gift, he said, an escape from the city. "You can have horses again," he said. "You'll love the quiet. You'll be able to concentrate on your writing."

And she did love it, at first. The horses carried her away and away through the desert, where she filled her lungs with the tang of sagebrush, her eyes with endless sky, the western mountains—sleeping volcanoes rising dark blue or snow-covered. Long nights full of shooting stars and love. The poems flowed from her like water after a thunderstorm. Back when fire season was three or four weeks at the end of summer—just until the autumn rains swept in.

But gradually, things dried up. Snowpack. Autumn rains. Thunderstorms, too—those intermittent light and sound shows prized for shifting the dial from broiling to cool. Now, the rumbling clouds are just a source of dread, of 50,000-degree sparks waiting to ignite the landscape in purifying flame.

The paint on the little house peels in long strips; bare wood shows gray like dirty underwear beneath. At thirty-four, Lena is showing wear, too. The dark hair, prematurely streaked with silver like her mother's, hangs limp over her shoulders. Crevices like empty creek beds line her hands. There, the ghost of a bruise, yellowed with time; another, darker, fresher, lurks beneath a sleeve. She hasn't written much—anything—for a while.

Drifting smoke turns the sun a dull orange, the incense of burning sage slips around the door, and her mother is there, across the table, worry etched in her tired face. Lena sees her more frequently these days, echoes of their conversations a tune stuck in her head.

Lena picks up her cup and sighs. "Don't start." She picks at a nail, broken and dirty.

"You know the signs: Time to get out."

"Just a shift in the wind. Nothing I have to do anything about."

"Ain't talking about the fires."

Lena feels the impatience in her mother's voice, the hint of desperation. Thoughts swirl, conceal, reveal a dull certainty lurking deep in her belly. She does know the signs. Time to run.

But where? Her friends have faded away out here with no Internet, cell phones a joke. The meetups with women she knows in Portland or Eugene never materialized. Something always came up; Mark would take off and leave her to care for the horses. Or her bruises would still be too fresh, too obvious, too hard to explain away to concerned faces.

She tries to resist the acrid prickle of smoke in the back of her throat, coughs.

"Don't make my mistake, baby. Any more of them, anyways."

"Your mistakes were your own, Mom." Lena's cup clatters down, empty. "Nothing to do with me."

"Mm hm."

The horses add their nervous whinnying to the voices in Lena's head. A kick rattles the paddock fence. She breathes in their panic; it joins her own in a rush up her spine. Time to run.

The radio crackles. An announcer's voice pierces the static: Level 3 evacuation, imminent danger, leave now—

She clicks the radio off. Stands too quickly, the empty room spinning. Three days since Mark stormed off, but the wildfire will bring him back. Any time now.

The fire pushes a tawny mass of smoke ahead of itself, rolling off the mountains, filling the valley, beating silently against the window. A flame shoots up, half a mile away. Then another, closer, as scattered trees catch wind-born embers and torch. Lines of fire snake through dry grass. Closer.

A hot draft touches her face, brings a low hum that throbs against her chest, electrifying the hair on her neck.

His truck is in the drive, oversized tires spitting gravel, shards of rock striking the window. Engine idling, growling, panting, eager to break the leash and be gone.

Her mother's voice, soft in her ear. "Run."

She hears the truck door slam. Hears the whiskey in his voice as he shouts her name. Hears his steps on the porch.

Too late, she looks for a hole to bolt through. Her gaze snags on the knife in the drainer.

Too late. Anger radiates from him as he stands in the doorway; she feels its heat on her face.

"Lena! What the fuck? Didn't you hear? They're evacuating us. Level 3!" He snaps on the radio, but a country song slides out: love is gone, too bad, so sad. "Christ, woman. Look outside!"

Hot wind swirls flakes of ash past the window, like dying moths.

Lena stumbles to the sink, slowly rinses out her coffee cup. Considers the knife, rejects it. Too dull. He'd told her to sharpen it, but she'd forgotten. His cast-iron pan sits there on the stove, though. She reaches for it, feels the weight as she lifts.

"You stupid bitch!" He grabs her arm.

The bruise he put there three days ago sings out, and she twists toward him; the heavy pan slams into the side of his head with the force of years.

Shocked into silence, he slides to the floor. Blood spatters the uneven boards. "Lena—"

But she's already moving. Out through falling embers to open the gate for the frantic horses. "Run!" she whispers.

She unleashes the truck, and it leaps forward. Galloping horses fly down the road ahead, leading her away and away. In the rearview, she sees Mark's face at the door, a wall of flame just behind, then shifts her gaze to the road ahead.

Gravel meets asphalt, and she shudders to a stop. Which way to go when the whole world is burning? She feels the heat on the back of her neck as the truck's radio oozes that same country song: too bad, so sad.

Lena smiles, clicks off the radio, and spins the wheel.

S. B. NOLEN (on Bluesky: @sbnolen.bsky.social; on Substack: https://sunolen.substack.com/) is a writer and photographer living in a multigenerational, multispecies household on the beautiful Kitsap Peninsula. After years of studying and writing about identity and motivation in social context, she now writes stories of women making space for themselves in the world. It's way more fun. Her work has appeared in *Circle of Seasons* and **Stone's Throw**.

OCTOBER 2025 PROMPT – During the month of October, the veil between the living and the dead is at its thinnest. This month, give us stories of haunted characters—either haunted by the remembrance of a lost loved one, or maybe haunted by the things they didn't do . . . or worse, the things they did do. Supernatural stories are okay (though not a requirement) in response to this prompt, but above all else, make it character-driven, and make it noir.

Like Silver

Derek Alan Jones

I stand leaning against a stone half-wall at the foot of granite stairs, in the same stance and spot I was in the first time that I saw her. It's the same stance and spot I've taken every night since they put her in the ground. I thumb the lighter she gave me after our first year together, and I touch the flame that springs from it to the tip of my cigarette.

I check my watch again after taking that first drag.

In just under a minute, the theater doors will open. The people will file through them, down the stairs, into the night. None of them will notice the woman walking along the edge of the crowd, who will brush by me so closely that I smell the rose oil she wears. In a city this size, a crowd like this, you never notice the ghosts.

She'll push her hair back with her hand and toss a smile over her shoulder at me, just the way she did on that first night we met.

Just the way she has every night since they put her in the ground.

Those doors finally open, and I flick my cigarette as the pounding in my chest tries to decide whether to stop or to double its pace.

Then, in the doorway, she's there.

In the marquee lights, she's silver. Not silver like the color, but silver like a Silver Age. Silver like the Silver Screen. Like hard lighting and soft focus. Like a perfect big band score.

She brushes by and as she does that rose scent hits me hard, and every ounce of will I have is put to work holding back the tears. The crowd is just a blur and a hum now. I'm mostly a blur myself. The only thing in focus is her. I watch her pass, and I breathe in every moment of her as it comes. I imagine that, if I hold my breath, I can hold on to those moments for just a little longer. I wait for the glance she'll give me and that playful cocked-brow smile. It's that smile that I still see in my head every time I hear her name.

But that smile doesn't come. Not tonight. Tonight, she does something she hasn't done in all the nights I've come here.

Tonight, she breaks the pattern.

She breaks her stride.

She stops and my heart stops with her, and when she turns and faces me fully, her eyes lock onto mine the way a hand locks around a throat. I cannot will myself to take a breath, and I cannot will myself to move, because the anger that burns in those eyes is one that she has never turned on me.

"You can't keep me here like this," she says, and her words are almost lost in my joy and heartbreak of hearing her voice. As they settle on me, though, the weight of those words is almost staggering.

I want to ask a question. I want to understand. But I can't clear my mind enough to decide what question it should be. Even if I could form the thought, I have no faith in my ability in that moment to form the words. Her face softens, but only slightly, when she speaks again.

"You have to see it all."

She's gone then, and my breath comes back in short and shallow stabs. I'm on my knees on the concrete, right arm flailing of its own accord, swatting at the hands of the man who tries to help me to my feet.

A few more breaths, and I'm running, without direction or intention, barely conscious of my movement, wanting only to put distance between myself and the words she said.

You have to see it all.

The cold stings my lungs, and the car exhaust thickens the air I'm choking on, but still I take it in gulps as I run in absolute disregard.

My limbs aren't under my control until I make it to my door, and even then, they shake so hard that I struggle to turn the key.

Once inside, her words play on a loop inside my head, and that look in her eye blazes through every inch of my memory.

You can't keep me here . . .

I'm not keeping her here, I tell myself. I know that it isn't true, but I keep up the act, as thin as it is, and I try and fail to convince myself.

I went to the theater that first night, when I should have been at her visitation, because I couldn't bring myself to tell the stories, or to hear the stories again. I didn't want to see her family. I didn't want to see the faces of our friends. Above all else, I didn't want to see her lying there like that. I didn't want that memory. I wanted to remember her the way she had been inside that perfect moment. I wanted things to be the way they were before it all went south.

I wanted to see her in silver.

I thought that I could cling to that image and spare myself the rest. So I went to the theater, and there she was. It was just as simple as that. I know she wouldn't have been there if I hadn't come to see. She wouldn't have come down those stairs every night if I hadn't been there waiting.

I take a long, slow pull from the bottle that sits on the kitchen counter, and, if only for a moment, the burn of that cheap bourbon chases everything else from my mind. That first pull leads to a second, and they multiply from there until my mind is no longer racing. Until it seems to stumble, and I do the same, down the hallway, to the bedroom, where the bottle I haven't noticed I'm still holding hits the floor.

She's not supposed to be here.

She's not supposed to be like this.

In the neon glow that has forced its way in through the crooked blinds, she looks the way a Lou Reed song sounds over second-hand speakers. Like a brash strum of a beaten guitar, or desperate words in a stilted voice that never quite finds the rhythm.

I run my eyes over the broad, feathered wings inked across her back, and I remember the way I wondered, the first time I saw them, if they were meant to be angel wings. By the time I saw her here, like this, though, I knew that didn't fit.

This was where it started. This was the first step she would take in her slow walk to the end. Even half-drunk and half in shock, I can see that now. What I can't see is how the hell I didn't understand it then.

It's all written out so clearly on every inch of her, and I'm sure that if she spoke a single word, I would hear it in her voice. I'd known her history and her old habits, but I let myself believe, or I made myself believe, that she was only tired and a little over-stressed. That some sleep and a decent breakfast would put the color back in that sunken face and the light back in those eyes.

I wonder then if this is what she meant by "see it all."

I don't have to fight the tears this time. I don't have to grind my teeth and close my throat to stifle the sobs. I'm almost entirely certain that I couldn't if I tried, so I let those tears and sobs come as they please, and I sink down to the carpet with my back against the wall.

It's there, on the floor, against the wall, that I find myself in the morning, and I'll admit that I'm grateful to the bourbon and shock for having dulled the night in my mind.

I don't get much time to relish that relief, though, because when I step out for a cigarette, she's waiting for me.

In the sunlight she is fading, sitting hunched and shaking in the corner of the balcony. Her knees are pulled up to her chest and tucked into a sweatshirt that I could swear used to fit her well. Her hair is down over the face that she refuses to turn toward me.

This was when I knew. This was when I finally let myself *admit* I knew. It was the last time we spoke, or at least the last time that I spoke to her. Spoke at her, maybe. For all my pleading, for all my demands, not a single word I said got through, and not a single word was returned. Even now, I can't piece together a sentence that would do either of us any good, but I search and I strain like I did then, begging my brain for anything that might prevent what's coming next, because I know, the same way I knew when I saw her like this, that she wouldn't make it through the day.

I blink and the corner's empty.

I light the first of seven Pall Malls I'll smoke before I can force myself inside.

When I do, it's there, where I knew it would be, sticking out from behind the counter – a pale and rigid hand lying still and flat against the carpet. My heart rips open all over again, but this time, I don't go to her. This time, I don't turn the corner to find the emptiness in her eyes and the needle still in her arm. I'm numb now, and I'm cold, and I can't help but wonder if this is the way she felt in the end. The words "see it all" scream in my head, but I can't make myself see this again.

Then, something breaks.

Something *must* have broken, somewhere inside my head, because I find myself sitting out on the front stoop, and I don't know or care in the moment exactly how I got there. The nails I've been digging into the concrete of those steps have worn down to the quick, and the taste of copper fills my mouth from chewing on my lip. The sun is warm on my face, and the air smells of late November, and I don't know how long I've been sitting there before I notice her next to me. This time, I'm the one who struggles to turn my eyes to her.

"I've seen it all," I tell her. "The beginning to the end."

She doesn't look at me when she answers.

"The beginning and the end were hardly all there was."

When I do look up, I find a trace of a laugh on her lips. Her hair is pulled haphazardly into an approximation of a bun, and strands of it fall over her face when she lets out that laugh. It's hearty and it's honest and her face is full of color and life. She turns that face up to the sun, and she pauses, and she basks in the light of it as if she were trying to breathe it in. This is the way I've seen her countless thousands of times. This is the her I had forgotten. The her I had overlooked. The one that I'd lost to the grief and the guilt and the infatuation and the ideals.

As she stands and disappears down those steps, I finally understand, because she isn't silver here. She isn't neon, or fading, or dead. Here, on this stoop, in the sunlight, all she is, is her.

I sit in that spot, silent and still, until the daylight gives way to the neon. In just under a minute, those theater doors will open, and the people will file through them, down the stairs, into the night.

But tonight, I won't be there waiting.

DEREK ALAN JONES spends most of his time working in a warehouse in Kansas and the rest of it writing speculative fiction. His work has appeared in the *Saturday Evening Post*, *Apex*, and *Tales to Terrify*, among others. Find it all at DerekAlanJones.com.

Virtue in a Boom Boom Room

AT Kessler

T he men come like bees to the hive, dripping honey between their Queen's legs, slick breasts, and sometimes, oddly, her hair. Their moans light up the room like napalm. Daddy said that our faith would be tested daily but *we must endure the worst to save the most*. Watching these men line up for pleasure, and watching their faces contort from fear to ecstasy, heats me up like the word of God. Flushed and tingling, I'm shocked by my own excitement. I know it's the devil trying to worm his pitchfork between my legs. But this ache and longing will not let up. I've worked hard to save Bui but now I understand it's the men souls that need saving - and maybe even my own.

Wanting to understand the mechanics of sex and to put into practice *enduring the worst to save the most*, I had asked Bui to let me observe her work. She agreed as long as I promised not to baptize her. Deal, but I will find a way to save her. Bui fascinates me. She insists that she is a businesswoman and these men are merely her clients. Once trapped by tradition, she is now trapped by war, yet this is the most autonomy she has had since leaving her village. There, she was expected to work all day like a water buffalo, feeding, shopping and cooking for her large family. Now, she works on her back, and sets her own hours. A real feminist, as Daddy would say. I do not judge her. Only God can.

One day while I was brushing her hair, Bui said, "When I was a young girl, I would rebury the bones of my Bà and Ông so that they could have a nice time in heaven. It was . . ." She paused, looking for the right word. ". . . not so much fun. And when the heavy monsoon rains come, the bones float up and I trip all over heads, arms, legs."

Looking down at the brush's pearlescent bone handle, I stopped brushing. An image filled my vision of a young Bui in pigtails, barefoot, playing in the rain as she skipped over her grandparents' bones, jutting out of the mud like stones in a stream.

"Hey!" she yelled, "keep brushing." I obeyed. "Now," she chuckled, "the men bury their bones in me so they too can have a bit of heaven. giống giống . . . same, same but different."

***

Sitting on a mat in the corner of Bui's room, notebook in hand, the men don't seem to mind my presence, when they notice me. Often, I don't think they even notice her, lost as they are in their lustful duties.

I used to look away. Lately, I watch these interactions with boredom. Even the most hideous sin can become mundane. I've started noticing the difference in the men's performances. Some thrust into Bui like jackrabbits, while others take it slow and ask her a lot of stupid questions like, "Do you like it like that?" I'm certain she does not. Some get rough. They pinch and slap and call her filthy names. Bui is placid and says nothing to further enrage these men, while I pray quietly: endure the worst to save the most, until they stop. I've observed over the past few months that these men are getting younger—as if Nixon is handing out draft orders along with high school diplomas—"Congratulations, you've graduated to Vietnam!"

It seems Nixon has wrung out the swamps and emptied farms of their sons and drafted them into almost certain death in Vietnam.

I'm here by choice and that fact allows me to have sympathy for these devils.

I take leave of Bui and her current client, who searches for her vagina like a pig rooting out a truffle. I pass by groups of soldiers running their beer cans across their foreheads in the sweltering heat. Most are drunk. Some dance slowly with bar girls. Others sit at the bar drinking and sweating. The GIs clap and whistle each time a bed frame hits the wall, knocking dust from the ceiling fan overhead.

The few regulars, journos and GIs, eye me wearily and step aside as I walk behind the bar to grab myself a Coca-Cola. I overhear one of them turn to his buddy, point at me and whisper, "Looks like mass is starting."

Ha, I think to myself. *It most certainly is, boys.*

Scooping up a handful of spicy peanuts from a filthy communal bowl, I walk over and yank out the jukebox's cord. Creedence Clearwater Revival abruptly shuts off. Everyone stares daggers at me as I stand on a table and preach fire and brimstone. Peanut dust flies out of my mouth like tiny missiles exploding on deaf ears.

"Save yourselves!" I boom at them. They mostly ignore me, but I catch one's eye. "You can hear me, brother. I know you can." He bows his head in shame.

The men jeer and throw peanuts at my head. "Hey, missionary girl," a scarecrow of a boy yells, "you know what you can feast on?" He grabs his crotch and laughs.

Another GI, with a face that could launch a thousand medivacs, joins in. "See if you can still pray with my Yankee Doodle in your mouth."

They high five each other and hurl the most vile and puerile insults at me. I use the bible as a shield to deflect them. Then out of the group steps a soldier, with an air of confidence as thick as the cigar smoke leaking out the sides of his mouth. "Davis" is sewn onto the breast pocket of his fatigues. He yells at the others to behave themselves in front of a lady.

"Ain't no ladies here," snorts a large man with a handlebar mustache and haunted eyes.

Davis gets in the man's face. "I said, watch your mouth in front of the lady."

Handlebar mustache pokes Davis in the chest, threatening him, "I only see one pussy here and that's you."

Smiling wildly, Davis puts his cigar out on the man's forehead. Handlebar Mustache shrieks. The other GIs hoot and holler. Someone throws a beer. A full-on fight breaks out. Bottles whoosh overhead and shatter on the tile floor. Davis grabs my hand and yells, "Run."

We dodge and weave through street hawkers and rickshaws and into a coffee shop, where we sit on brightly colored plastic chairs across from one another. We are both laughing and trying to catch our breath. Looking at him, I see that he's actually younger than I first thought, maybe only a few years older than my twenty years. His thick framed glasses and black bushy eyebrows give him a Groucho Marx quality. Daddy would surely whip me if he knew I was out with a GI.

Davis orders from the waitress in flawless Vietnamese. She is as surprised as I am. "Not every day you hear a dink order in Vietnamese," he winks. "What's your name?"

"Gloria."

"Like the song."

He whistles that dang Van Morrison song, which usually makes me cringe, but he's so out of tune that it's charming.

"So, Gloria," he drops his head into his hands like an excited schoolgirl waiting for her friend to divulge a delicious secret, "what's a girl like you doing spreading the gospel in a boom-boom room in Saigon?"

Before I can answer, the waitress interrupts our conversation with a plate of something that resembles peanut brittle.

"Try this," he says excitedly. "It's called keo cu do."

The keo cu do glistens. It tastes like home, like Tennessee.

"It's better than spreading—"

"Your legs?"

"The gospel!" I fold my arms over my chest to communicate my displeasure at his crudeness.

"Why don't you tell me about yourself?" He wipes sugar from my lips and I find myself wondering if he tastes as sweet as this unpronounceable Vietnamese peanut brittle.

Stop it, I tell myself. These thoughts are dangerous and dirty—so deliciously dirty.

"Well, I guess you could say that I'm here on a spiritual internship."

"Spiritual internship," Davis laughs. "I like that. Like a spiritual tour of duty. Most of the men in my unit start off as men but leave as spirits. Kinda like you, they intern, but in the afterlife."

I'm attuned to the cynicism behind his humor. And cynicism, like a sin, only blackens your soul.

I shall not give into it. I will save you, Davis.

"So, Gloria, how many have you saved?"

"It's not a numbers game," I try my best to explain. "You know, we aren't that different." I sip my coffee and study the amused look on Davis's face. "We are both soldiers sent here on a mission. I'm on a mission to save souls, just as you are here on a mission to stamp out communism."

Davis slaps the table. "Onward Christian soldier! But aren't you afraid? Hell, I'm afraid every god damned day, sorry."

I gently take Davis's hand in mine. "It's not for me to decide. God has a plan, even for you." Leaning in so close that our noses are practically touching, I whisper the only question that matters. "Davis, have you been saved? Have you accepted Christ's love?" Slowly, I pull my hand from his, our fingers lightly hooking as I let go.

"No. And the only thing you need to save me from is a second serving of keo cu do." Seeing my dismay, he changes tack. "Look, Gloria, I appreciate your concern over my mortal coil. But I need protection, not saving."

"I can't offer you physical protection, but I can offer spiritual protection."

Davis's smile fills his face. Did I say something funny?

"If spiritual protection keeps me out of a glad bag, then sure."

Frowning at his sarcasm, I'm about to admonish him when there is a loud banging on the window. Turning toward the sound, we see Handlebar Mustache and a few of the GIs from the bar beating fists on the window and pointing at us through the glass.

"Gloria," Davis says, waving at our waiting assailants, "I think it's time we go."

We knock over the table as we run past them. Davis is practically dragging and cheering me on to run faster. Looking over my shoulder, I see Handlebar Mustache and friends are closing in, maybe 100 yards away, when I feel a wave of hot air like the devil blowing his fetid breath on my face, followed by a thunderclap. The shockwave knocks me into Davis and sends us tumbling to the ground, somersaulting towards Armageddon, until we come to a stop. The world disconnects.

A pinhole of light breaks through my vision; my nostrils fill with the smell of sulfur. Silence is replaced by a high-pitched ringing in my ears. Opening my eyes, I see the walking wounded dazed and bleeding, men and women turned inside out, cars flipped over, and a large smoking hole where, just moments ago, shop-houses stood. Davis stands over me yelling something I can't hear. A stream of blood runs down his temple and pools in his shirt's collar. Davis shakes me. I flop between his hands like a rag doll. Then he slaps me back to reality.

Immediately, I jump up to flee because Handlebar and friends are going to catch us. I'm frantic. Davis drapes his body over mine like a blanket, muffling my screams.

I'm covered in his blood. "You are hurt?"

"It's nothing." He grimaces, pulling a piece of glass from the side of his head.

I look down at the mangled corpses of our pursuers. Bloody confetti spill out of their torsos; their body parts are scattered amongst the fruit and vegetables from upturned carts. And I think, fleetingly, who will bury and rebury their bones?

The scene is so incomprehensible that I start laughing uncontrollably.

Davis looks around nervously. "Shh, you are in shock. We should get somewhere safe. And we need to go now, chuckles. Ok? Let's walk, soldier. On your feet."

Davis's cool is unfathomable. I can only guess at what he's witnessed on the battlefield to so calmly move us through the carnage while wounded. Davis steers me past Bui's bar when I notice that the street is missing a tooth. There is a smoking crater where the bar once stood. The bar is gone. Bui is gone.

Breaking free of Davis, I run towards the burning bar, slipping in viscera.

"Bui," I yell into the smoking hole of twisted metal. The guilt from not saving her knocks me to my knees. The world goes black.

I wake up on the street next to Davis.

"And she's back." His eyes are unfocused. "Congrats, chuckles. You survived your first bombing. How's it feel?" He slurs his words, woozy from blood loss.

I fear he will die. I know what I need to do.

He smiles at me weakly as I baptize him in his own blood.

AT KESSLER is a writer and documentary producer living in Southern California with her husband, son, and two dogs. When not writing or on set, she can be found in her garden battling aphids. Her writing has appeared in the anthology *Six Word Memoir* and online.

DECEMBER 2025 PROMPT – The office holiday party is the setting for this month's **Stone's Throw** prompt. What happens when you're forced into a social setting with a bunch of people you would never willingly socialize with except for a paycheck? How does dipping into a less formal space embolden your protagonist to tell Jan from Accounting what they really think of her? What hare-brained schemes can your protagonist come up with after knocking back a few cold ones and eyeing up the unguarded bank safe? And what fresh hell and awkward hangovers await the story's characters the morning after?

Santa Daddy

James D.F. Hannah

The afternoon of Christmas Eve, and Slater's at a dive bar on Crenshaw, drinking well bourbon and eating un-sauced wings—both keto—and hoping Chloe, the deeply-tattooed bartender, will take him home with her when her shift's over, because he's been living in his car since his girlfriend found those photos of him with her sister on his phone, and sleeping in his Prius is fucking his back.

That's when Ashlynn shows up. Or rather, Ashlynn's chest announces her entrance, and the rest of her appears over time, a royal procession of tits and hips and ass. She's a spank bank wish list: four-figure blonde hair, five-figure rack, Brazilian butt lift, cheekbones that are a cutting hazard. A smoke show that should require a warning from the Forestry Service.

She clicks four-inch heels across the concrete floor in time to Darlene Love on the jukebox.

Chloe gives her the look. "Get you something, honey? Beer? Wine? Antibiotics?"

Ashlynn ignores her, slides into a booth. Slater chews the last bit of meat off a drumette and carries his drink over.

"I've got a job," she tells him. "Thought you could use the money."

Slater tries to play it cool, but Ashlynn is . . . not wrong. He's struggled since he left the industry, looking for mainstream work. He can't score more than a day player gig on a third-tier Netflix series, and he tells himself it's because there's prejudice still against porn, and not because there are more images of his junk on the Internet than there are cat videos.

He's made ends meet during the holidays playing Santa Claus. Buff Santa, though. Saint Nick with his swole on. For late-year bachelorette parties, or girl-boss holiday get-togethers where Slater can strip and grind to "Last Christmas."

As good as the money is, though, the biggest benefit is the shocking number of women who want to fuck Santa Claus. And why wouldn't they? Slater's six-two, gym-ripped the way he was shooting scenes in Griffith Park. His sleeveless red velvet costume and the mischievous twinkle in his eye scream to these ladies he's waiting to come down their chimneys.

But this year's he's been SOL—Santa outta luck. Demand's down for a Father Christmas who's more of a "Daddy." Work-from-home has blown up office festivities, and bachelorette parties, they'd rather drunk pedal than paw at a chiseled Kris Kringle and wine-drunk whisper if the stockings are the only things that are hung.

"I'm not filming anymore," Slater says.

"It's not a scene. I've got a corporate party tonight, and my Santa got busted shooting with girls with fake IDs."

"My dad did always say fifteen'll get you twenty. What's the job?"

"Tech bros at Silicon Beach. They're taking a break from doing ketamine and kissing oligarch ass to celebrate the birth of Christ."

"And you're planning to rob them?"

Ashlynn rolls a violet contact-lensed eye.

"Duh. Interested?"

Slater tells himself he should go home with Chloe. She's the only reason he's got well bourbon to drink and chicken wings to eat. She's sweet and funny, owns her own house that's probably decorated for the holidays. Plus, he doesn't want to wake up on Christmas morning in the parking lot of a Planet Fitness.

Still, he's not surprised when he tells Ashlynn, "Sure, I'm in."

***

That evening, Slater drives to a mansion in the Palisades, where the interior design is best described as "asshole luxe." Everything's cavernous and blindingly white and Slater half-expects Tom Cruise to cable down from the ceiling. There's a DJ doing a drum-and-bass mix of "Baby It's Cold Outside" and naked women being used as sushi tables. Dudes outnumber ladies ten to one, the women gorgeous and bored, obviously hired to keep the party from being a complete sausage fest, while the guys roam about like coked-out hyenas.

Ashlynn's costume is a fur-lined red negligee and G-string with garters and hose and heels. She's talking to a guy with powder around his nostrils and roided muscles straining the seams of a shirt sized for a ten-year-old. She introduces him as the party host, Reggie.

"Call me Biff," he says.

"No," Slater says. "So what do you do, Reggie? Marry and murder rich widows?"

Biff flashes very white, very expensive teeth.

"I made an app for guys to track down women who ghost them. After that company went public, I rolled the money into shorting subprime loans. Now I invest in AI."

"I liked you better thinking you killed old ladies," Slater says.

Biff's not listening. His eyes are locked on a redheaded bombshell strolling by in an LBD.

"End of the night, you two hand out the holiday bonuses," he says, gesturing to a stack of small white boxes, each tied with an elaborate red ribbon. "Help yourself to the food and the booze. Coke's by the caviar. Ketamine's next to the gingerbread cookies." He walks toward the bombshell. "Don't get them confused."

Ashlynn says to Slater, "Biff found me on OnlyFans. He acts all alpha, but twice a week he puts on a puppy mask and lets me whip his bare ass."

"Then you know what's in the boxes?" Slater says.

"Crypto wallets. Each one loaded with six figures, every penny untraceable. Biff was barking, he was so excited to tell me. I went home and made a dozen identical boxes. They're stashed under the gift table. When it's time, I'll hand you a box, and you give it to the next asshole in line. Every few boxes, I'll switch one of mine for a real one. Everyone'll be wasted by then, so they won't notice, and we'll haul ass out of here."

Slater nods and checks across the room. Biff's trapped the bombshell in a corner, talking, not noticing her eyes have gone dead.

Not *completely* dead, however. because she's eye-fucking Slater. Her smile is feral.

Santa freak.

It's on.

Slater turns on his Santa voice. Says to Biff, "What do we have here? Getting ready for Santa?"

Biff snarls, "Fuck off, Saint Nick."

"Now, now, you don't want on the naughty list, do you?"

Biff squares up. Slater recognizes fight training from a gym. Doubts Biff's ever had a brawl where a check didn't secure the outcome.

Slater slaps his hand on Biff's shoulder, lets his thumb find the right nerve, digs in. Biff's knees wobble and sweat pours from the line of hair plugs trenched across the top of his brow.

"Jingle your jolly ass elsewhere, Reggie," Slater says. No holiday tone now. He releases his grip and Biff collapses against the wall.

"Skank," Biff says to the bombshell, and storms off toward the caviar.

The bombshell bites on the skinny red straw from her drink.

"Thanks, Santa." She takes the straw and traces the unchewed end along the edge of Slater's tricep. Bites her bottom lip. Gets close enough, her perfume hits the "reset" button in Slater's brain, flushing all of his blood south.

"You know," she says, soft and breathy, "I think I'm awfully naughty."

She goes to a catering table, grabs a bottle of wine and a corkscrew. A wink and a shake of ass and vanishes down a hallway.

Slater sees Ashlynn talking with two guys, giving a tour de force performance of someone who gives a fuck what they have to say. Decides he's got time, pops a blue pill from his pocket, goes to find the bombshell.

He finally finds her in the library, where the books have uncracked spines and everything's crusted in oak and gold leaf like dried cold sores. Southern California and there's a fireplace, for fuck's sake.

The bombshell's draped across a desk the size of a basketball court, a come-hither expression on her face which has Slater hithering in her direction, the rip of Velcro closures, his costume dropping to the floor. He feels a surge of heat through his body, both the thrill of fucking in a place like this, and probably the blue pill.

The bombshell tells him to keep the beard on.

They twist and shape one another's bodies across the desk surface, their noises drowned out by the DJ trying his damndest to make Leonard Cohen's "Hallelujah" into not just a Christmas song, but one you can dance to.

Finally, the bombshell explodes, a piercing scream that echoes between the walls, muting Slater's smaller, more guttural sounds. They collapse onto the desk, and Slater offers to open the bottle of wine.

He's got the corkscrew, reaching for the bottle, when the library door opens and Biff says, "I'm paying you to do a job, not—"

A beat. Then.

"That was my grandfather's desk!"

Biff runs to the fireplace and grabs a poker. Slater can see the rage in his eyes, the fury of a desire he's been denied, as well as the fresh Colombian snowfall dusting his nose.

As soon as Biff's close enough, before he's got a chance to swing the poker, Slater throws a punch.

This is the very moment Slater remembers he's holding the corkscrew.

Biff drops the poker, and his shirt turns red as blood pours from around the corkscrew lodged in his neck.

(Slater later learns from the ME's report that he hit Biff's carotid artery. "A one-in-a-million punch," it claims. Lucky him. It's also where he learns the word "exsanguination.")

The bombshell's screams draw a crowd, and if nothing else it gets the DJ to stop playing. Everyone has a cell phone out, either recording for social media or calling 911—but mostly for social media. Biff's very dead on the floor, lying in the middle of a—fuck you not—zebra skin rug. Real zebra.

The cops arrive, pissed to leave the Korean barbecue joint feeding them, having to deal with this shit on Christmas Eve. Slater tries to find Ashlynn in the chaos, but can't. She's gone, and, he realizes, so is every single one of those goddamn Christmas bonus boxes.

As he's getting handcuffed, Slater thinks, *I should have gone home with Chloe.*

JAMES D.F. HANNAH (on Instagram / Threads @jamesdfhannah; on Bluesky @jamesdfhannah.bsky.social) is the author of the Shamus Award-winning Henry Malone series, including the novels *Behind the Wall of Sleep* and *Because the Night*. His work has been nominated for the Anthony Award and the Pushcart Prize and his short fiction has appeared in *Best American Mystery and Suspense*; *Ellery Queen Mystery Magazine*; *Eight Very Bad Nights*, edited by Tod Goldberg; *Playing Games*, edited by Lawrence Block; ***Under the Thumb: Stories of Police Oppression***, edited by S.A. Cosby; *Vautrin*; ***Rock and a Hard Place***; *Dark Yonder*; and *The Anthology of Appalachian Writers*. He lives in Louisville, Kentucky, where the bourbon is.

COLD CALLER
Purveyors of fine crime
and mystery fiction.
"A totally legitimate enterprise."
coldcallermag.substack.com

DNDP is a home for writers who fall into the in-between: too genre for the literary world, but too literary for most genre publications. We champion fiction that sits in the gaps, and publish work that can only be called what it is—

like **a dog named Dog**

See our Submission Guidelines

www.dognameddogpress.com

EDITORIAL BIOGRAPHIES

MORGAN SULLIVAN (*Stone's Throw* Editor; Bluesky: @the-bigleblueski.bsky.social) is a writer of fiction, comedy, and letters to the editor. A recent East Coast transplant, she is enjoying the trees that aren't on fire. Her writing has been featured at *Fireside Fiction Magazine*, *Shotgun Honey*, and *Tough*, as well as in the *Killing Malmon* and *Murder-A-Go-Go's* anthologies. She has also published an erotic story about a ham sandwich. True story. You can track her down over at govneh.com.

JAY BUTKOWSKI (*Stone's Throw* Annual Editor; Threads / IG: @jtbutkowski) is a writer of fiction, an eater of tacos and an amateur pizzaiolo who lives in New Jersey. His stories have appeared in online and print publications, including *Shotgun Honey*, *Dark Yonder*, *Tough*, *Yellow Mama*, *All Due Respect*, and *Vautrin*, among others. He is a founding editor at **Rock and a Hard Place Press**, an independent publisher chronicling "bad decisions and desperate people." He's also a father of teenage twins, a doting husband, and a middling pancake chef.

ROGER NOKES (RHP Editor-in-Chief; Threads / IG: @StantonMcCaffery) writes fiction under the pseudonym Stanton McCaffrey. His short stories have been featured in *Tough*, *Reckon Review*, *Dark Yonder*, *Mystery Tribune*, *Vautrin*, *Shotgun Honey*, *Guilty Crime Story Magazine*, and more. He has published two novels: *Into* *the Ocean*; and **Neighborhood of Dead Ends**. His short story, "Will I See The Birds When I Am Gone," was featured in *Best American Mystery and Suspense 2024*.

ALBERT TUCHER (Contributing Editor; Facebook: @albert.tucher) is the creator of sex worker Diana Andrews, who has appeared in more than 100 hardboiled stories in venues including *The Best American Mystery Stories 2010*. Her first longer case, the novella *The Same Mistake Twice*, was published in 2013. In 2017, Albert Tucher launched a second series set on the Big Island of Hawaii, in which *Pele's Prerogative* is the latest entry. He is a past president of the Mystery Writers of America NY Chapter, lives in New Jersey, and loves NJ Turnpike jokes.

PAUL J. GARTH (Editor; Threads / IG: @PauljGarth) has been published in *Thuglit, Tough, Needle: A Magazine of Noir, Plots with Guns, Crime Factory*, **Rock and a Hard Place Magazine**, and several other anthologies and web magazines. His novella, *The Low White Plain*, part of the "A Grifter's Song" series, was released in June 2022. He writes in Nebraska, where he lives with his family.

ROB D. SMITH (Editor; Threads / IG: @RobertDominicSmith) is a common man attempting to write uncommon fiction from Louisville, KY. Regarded for darkly humanizing fiction, his story "A Box Full of Soul" was selected for *The Best American Mystery & Suspense 2025*. Rob's Anthony Award-nominated debut thriller *Good-Looking Ugly* is available from Shotgun Honey. His fiction has appeared in *Apex Magazine, Reckon Review, Thriller Magazine, Vautrin, Dark Yonder, Tough*, and several other crime, horror, and speculative magazines, anthologies, and online publications. Find his work at https://robdsmith.carrd.co/.

ASHLEY-RUTH M. BERNIER's (Acquisition Editor; Threads / IG: @armbernier) work has appeared in *Ellery Queen's Mystery*

Magazine, Black Cat Weekly, **Stone's Throw**, Smoking Pen Press, *Malice Domestic's Mystery Most Devious* and *Mystery Most Humorous, The Best American Mystery and Suspense 2023,* and other esteemed anthologies. Originally from St. Thomas, U.S. Virgin Islands, Ashley-Ruth writes mysteries highlighting the vibrant culture of her home. Her first novel length work is forthcoming from Crooked Lane Books in 2026. She currently lives with her family and teaches first grade in North Carolina.

VICTOR DE ANDA (Acquisition Editor; Bluesky: @victorde anda.bsky.social) is a movie geek and music freak who enjoys writing stories. His fiction has been published in *Dark Waters Vols. 1 & 2, Mystery Tribune, Shotgun Honey, Yellow Mama,* and *Punk Noir Magazine,* with more forthcoming. His story "Bad Man Down" has been included in *The Best American Mystery and Suspense 2025,* edited by Don Winslow and Steph Cha. He can be found living in the suburbs of Philadelphia. Find him online at www.victordeanda.com.

SUSAN JESSEN (Acquisition Editor; Threads / IG: @SuzJay11) enjoys reading, reviewing, and writing fiction of various genres. She received an MFA in Writing Popular Fiction from Seton Hill University. A former Priority Editor at *Flash Fiction Magazine,* she continues to provide editorial feedback during their quarterly contests. Her flash fiction has been published under a pseudonym in anthologies and magazines such as *The Arcanist, Lost Balloon,* and *Shotgun Honey.*